# THE SOUND OF SILENCE

## SHEILA QUIGLEY

burgess
books

www.theseahills.co.uk

ISBN-13:9780992878429

Printed and bound by
BOOKS & CATALOGUES LTD, S63 4DB

Burgess Books
Houghton-le-Spring
United Kingdom
www.theseahills.co.uk

# DEDICATION

for Janette Husband

(you know why)

# THE SOUND OF SILENCE

## PROLOUGE

It was a loud thud just above his head that woke him up. With no idea where he was, or how he had even got here, he only knew that it was pitch black and he could barely move. He tried to blink, once, twice, then rapidly, and couldn't understand why his eyelids wouldn't open. And why the only thing he could smell was the musty tang of damp earth.

He lifted his hand to rub at his eyes, and his body jerked in shock as the sound came again. He'd heard that same sound recently but couldn't remember where. With his heart beat starting to race, he lifted his hand and suddenly whacked it against something which felt like wood just above his head, his body shivered with fear when he realised there was nowhere left for his hand to go. He brought his other hand up and pushed at whatever was blocking it, his whole body jumped when the sound came again; then he froze as icy fingers covered him from head to foot, his bladder emptied, but he felt no remorse, or embarrassment, only an ever growing fear. Fear that he was right.

He ran his tongue around his dry lips; his heart beat began to double, as slowly memory came back. He started to yell as loudly as he could.

'Help…Help me…Please somebody help me.'

'Please.' His words reduced to a pitiful begging.

He rubbed his eyes again, this time realising that some sort of tape was covering them, finding the edge, he ripped hard and the tape came off, once the sting died down he heaved a sigh of relief and rested his head for a moment.

Placing his elbows at his side he pushed hard against the wood above him, but even though he was a strong man he couldn't budge whatever was on top of him. He began to yell again, over and over for help, until his throat was sore. He refused to let his mind dwell on where he was, but slowly like a worm, the thought wriggled into his brain.

'Please help me God.' He whispered as tears ran down his face.

But there was no answer, for nothing is as silent as the grave.

SUNDAY

# CHAPTER ONE

'No,' she screamed from the bottom of the stairs. 'I hate you. Hate you...Hate you.' Each word was accompanied by a fist slammed into the back of the baby's highchair; the third slam knocked the chair over, where it bounced on the floor.

'Change the record Sarah,' her father shouted back.

The woman lying next to him opened her eyes. 'Not again,' she muttered, then with a groan turned over and pulled the lemon duvet over her body, and tightly closed her eyes.

'And I hate you an 'all.' Sarah yelled. 'I know you're awake, but just ignore me like you always do, cos I'm not your fucking precious son... Am I?'

'Sarah,' this time her father really shouted at her. 'I will not have you talking like that about your mother.'

With a heavy sigh, the woman Rose Sinclair, pulled the duvet over her head and buried her face in the pillow.

'Mother! Some fucking mother she is. The bitch doesn't even know she's got two kids. I hate her and I hate you, and that horrible shit, stinking, bastard kid.'

Sarah swept her hand over the dishes in the drying wrack.

Rose started to cry when the sound of dishes crashing into the sink reached them.

The battles with their fourteen year old daughter had been going on for over a year, ever since the birth of baby Thomas. Sarah had changed from a sweet loving girl to a monster. Rose had long suspected drugs, but her husband Gregg wouldn't hear of it, not his darling little Sarah, no way! He just kept insisting over and over that it was jealousy over the new baby, and that her hormones would be acting up.

Excuse, after excuse, Rose thought, as she tried to burrow deeper into the bed.

'I hate you all...Fuck you.' The shout was followed by the slamming of the front door, and the cry of the baby.

Rose groaned as she pulled the duvet down and looked at the clock. Six thirty, slowly she slipped her legs out of the bed and reached for her dressing gown.

'I'll go.'

Gratefully Rose slumped back down on the bed. A moment later her husband Gregg came back with a smiling baby Thomas. Rose sat up and reached for him, like his sister, Thomas shared the brown hair and green eyes that both of his parents had.

As Thomas was drifting back to sleep, Rose said. 'We have to get help it can't go on any longer- something's wrong with her. Apart from being the obviously spoilt brat she's turned into. For a fact the neighbours will be complaining soon.'

'Really-seeing as the nearest neighbour is more than a hundred yards away, I doubt it.'

Rose glared at him. 'You are wrong, she must be on something. She has everything she wants, more than what she needs and a hell of a lot more than most kids her age. For fuck's sake she's just come back from a skiing trip.' Her voice started to rise, sensing his mothers mood, Thomas started to cry again.

Gregg looked from his wife's face to his son.

'Okay, you're right;' he sighed deeply, it was time to face up to it there was something wrong with their daughter. 'I'll pull a few favours in and make an appointment for today, suppose we have to drag her there.'

'Good, and no listening to her screaming and threatening she'll phone child line or social services.'

Nodding, and seeing that sleep was not an option anymore, Gregg went into the on suite to shower before work.

## CHAPTER TWO

She was sitting on a wooden kitchen chair, naked, with her legs tied to each front chair leg and her hands tied behind her back. The room was in darkness, all she could see was him-also naked, moving slowly towards her.

Her heart was pounding; sweat was running into her eyes. Never in her whole life had she felt so helpless, so frightened. She began to rock from side to side, hoping that she would fall before he reached her and the chair would break, at the very least freeing her legs.

Suddenly she stopped rocking, there was someone behind her, she felt something slide around her throat, she couldn't move her head, whatever was round her neck kept on getting tighter. She screamed, and tried to move her head to the right. The noose or whatever it was tightened; she screamed again, she felt herself begin to choke. Panicking again she flung her body from side to side. Suddenly she was being pulled forward by a pair of strong arms and the noose disappeared.

'Lorraine, Lorraine. Wake up. Wake up.'

Detective Inspector Lorraine Hunt opened her eyes. Her hand touched her throat, pulling long strands of her blonde hair away from her neck, confused she sat up quickly. 'What...Where?'

'You've been dreaming again, your hair was wrapped around your throat; don't know how you didn't strangle yourself.' Her partner, Detective Sergeant Luke Daniels, put his arm around her. Tall dark skinned and handsome Luke turned many a head, but his heart was locked with Lorraine's.

'I need the bathroom, now.' Lorraine pushed him away and quickly got out of bed.

In the bathroom, she leaned against the door and breathed deeply until her head cleared. She moved to the sink and looked at herself in the mirror. Her long blonde hair hung past her shoulders, and there were deep shadows underneath her blue eyes.

Resisting the urge to smash the mirror with her fist, she rinsed the flannel with cold water and washed her face.

Why can't I get it out of my mind? She thought, staring at herself again.

The bastard!

Lorraine had been attacked by a serial killer three months ago, tied up naked and fearing she was about to be raped at the very least, she had struggled free and managed to overcome him. The case was in Durham crown court on Monday but the closer the date got the worse it affected her.

Going back in to the bedroom she shook her head at Luke as he reached out for her. 'Come back to bed love.'

No, I'm awake now Luke. We'll be getting up in an hour or so anyhow.'

'More like two.' Luke looked at the clock as Lorraine slipped her dressing gown on.

'I don't want to be late on my first day back, do I? Go back to sleep.'

Luke flopped back on the bed and stared at the ceiling. About to say come back to bed again, he closed his mouth as he heard the door close.

Down stairs Lorraine, got a can of diet coke out of the fridge and sat on the settee. Switching the television on she watched the news channels for the next thirty minutes, unable to concentrate she kept flicking from one channel to the other, as the rain beat steadily against the windows.

## CHAPTER THREE

Robbie Lumsdon, wriggled out from underneath his bed, crawled across the dark blue bedroom carpet to his brother Darren's bed, a shrine to Sunderland football club, and wriggled under there. He searched every inch of the floor space and was slithering back out, when his hand touched something sticky, he raised his hand to his face and smelt the dark looking matter.

'Oh you dirty scruffy bastard.' He was shaking his hand free of the remains of a three day old pizza, when a sudden light thump landed in the middle of his back.

'What you doing creep?'

Out from under the bed, Robbie looked up to find Darren hanging over the edge of the bed staring at him, his face two inches above his. Darren's skin was a few shades darker than the rest of the family, and his eyes were brown. Robbie pushed Darren away and sat up. 'I'm looking for me friggin phone, doughnut head. Instead I found this,' he rubbed his hand on Darren's arm. 'What do you think I'm doing?'

Looking at the marks on his arm, Darren shrugged. 'Again?'

'Aye.'

'But you looked under there yesterday. How come you didn't see the pizza then?'

'Unbelievable-and get that mess picked up, anyhow just thought I'd have another look.'

'Did you have a dream telling you where to find it?'

'Err...No. Thicko.'

'They do on that telly programme.'

Robbie groaned. 'What you been watching now?'

Darren shrugged and scratched his armpit. 'Dunno, but mam and Sandra were glued to it the other day like.'

Robbie picked one of Darren's footballs up and threw it at him. 'Don't believe everything you see on the telly.'

Catching the ball, Darren laughed as he got out of bed and stretched. 'You'll not see that phone again mate, it'll be sold on by now, guaranteed.'

'Guess you're right.' In a foul mood, unusual for Robbie, he left the bedroom, snaffled a piece of toast out of his sister Claire's hand and left for work, as yelling her head off, Claire woke the rest of the Lumsdon family up.

## CHAPTER FOUR

Thirteen miles away, Fiona Max-Philips pushed her two children, fourteen year old Oliver and ten year old Molly, quickly up the path to the house to avoid the black clouds which seemed to have appeared the moment they had got out of the taxi. Already she was not thinking much of the outside of the house, in fact she thought. It's disgusting.

The battered front door was painted a sickly green with peeling paint showing a dark red undercover, as if the door had been repeatedly slashed by a knife welding maniac, and blood from his victim was seeping through. And with what looked like dirty pink curtains up at the windows, although with all the grime on them the true colour was debatable, the curtains were drawn tightly together at the windows, allowing no view of what was inside.

Please God let it be better inside, she thought, with a sinking heart as she took the key chain, with slightly trembling fingers, out of the pocket of her brown leather designer jacket. She fiddled for a moment finding the right one, before inserting it into the lock which opened smoothly. Quickly she glanced up, then down the street before following her children through into the house and locking the door and the first drops of rain behind her. For a moment she leaned against the wall, took a deep breath, and wishing a moment later that she had not, then letting the stale air out of her lungs and wondering what she was about to face, she squared her shoulders and walked through into the sitting room.

A natural redhead with shimmering green eyes, she tucked her shoulder length curly hair behind her ears, before taking a packet of tissues out of her pocket and handing them to Molly, who was still sniffing from a recent bout of the flu. She stared at her children for a moment, knowing she would die before letting any harm come to them. They were innocents in all of this. Her oldest child, sixteen year old Liam, was in intensive care at Newcastle hospital, having been flown there from York, where he had been trampled on by a rogue horse on a visit to the stables with his father. An as yet unexplained accident and one they wouldn't get to the bottom of until Liam regained conscious. No one had come forward yet to say they had seen what had really happened, from what they did know Liam, full of excitement, had apparently gone on ahead to the stables to visit their beloved horse Flame, who was running his first ever race later in the day, because Fiona's husband had been talking to an old friend. When he and his friend finally reached the stables it was to find Liam curled up in a ball, with a strange horse hovering next to him.

But deep in her heart, Fiona knew that it had been no accident, it had been a warning.

But why the hell my Liam? She asked herself again, why not her husband or her brother in law or was it as the police had thought at the time, just a case of the wrong place and the wrong time. And they still thought that, because there had been no contact at all since the supposed accident, no demands, nothing.

But they could have deliberately targeted Liam to show that they did mean business.

'Couldn't they have?' She muttered.

'Mum!' Her daughter's voice shocked her out of her reverie. Molly, plump with beautiful dimples and who had inherited her mother's colouring, and who for the past three months had insisted that everything she wore was various shades of green, wailed as she waved her arms dramatically around in the air. 'Look at it mum…It's a dump. Horrible…Horrible, mum…I don't want to live here. And the smell…How can I bring my friends to this…This dump?' She stamped her right foot, as her voice grew louder. 'Do something mum...I want to go home- you said it would be fun, but it's not, it's...It's horrible.'

Fiona's eyes followed her daughter's hands, her heart sinking, for a safe house it looked as if it could fall down at any moment.

She flicked the light switch on the wall by the door, and as she'd suspected it got worse, much worse.

'What's that smell?' Oliver tall for his age, his dark hair cropped close to his skull, and a mirror image of his brother Liam, and their father, asked, as he kicked an empty lager can right across the dark wooden floor, it ended up hitting the skirting board with a dull ping, and leaving a scratch among the many others.

Molly wrinkled her nose. 'Poo it stinks...mum- I don't like it here, I really don't like it...Why can't we go home?'

'Because...'

Molly looked up at her mother, her face demanding an answer. When her mother didn't reply, she asked again. 'Because why mum?'

Fiona sighed, wanting to scream at Molly to stop her winging, instead she took a bottle of water out of her bag and taking a sip she choose to ignore her daughters question. She guessed that some druggie low life's or, and alkies, had broken in and spent more than a few nights here.

But it should have been checked out before we moved in, for God's sake!

Fucking useless bloody police!

'We would have been better off staying at the boarding house, at least it was clean. And a very much better district than this despicable place!' She muttered under her breath, as Molly looked at her with a puzzled frown on her face, her green eyes starting to fill up with tears. Fiona hated bad language and frowned whenever she heard it, but for the first time in her life she realised, what a relief it could be.

The room was medium sized, with a large bay window, and she guessed that the cream leather settee with matching chairs, had once been in good condition, but now it had slash marks which looked quite fresh all over it, with the dark grey stuffing tumbling out. One of the two chairs was upside down, with a gaping hole where the bottom covering should be. Broken glass littered the dark green rug in front of the fireplace, and the pink curtains were worse than ghastly, and she was not impressed with the plain white walls covered in odd shaped red dots amongst the filthy graffiti.

She dropped the suitcase and with a tingling feeling running up her spine, moved closer to the wall. She stared for a moment and realised her suspicions were right.

Fuck! She thought. It is blood, what the?

How dare they put my family here?

She lifted a finger to trace the markings, then with a shiver she pushed her hand deep into her pocket.

'I don't like it here mum.' Molly said again, her eyes wide as she stared at the wall.

'It's alright darling.' Fiona patted her daughter's arm. 'We'll Get it sorted.'

'It's blood!' Oliver, his dark eyes wide, squealed, as he came in from upstairs. 'Ugh, I'm not stopping here any longer, it's creepy, and that just might be someone's brains on the wall, gross..! And don't ever go upstairs.'

'Oliver!'

Oliver shrugged. 'There's some writing on the walls, in all the bedrooms, bad writing...And it stinks...Wait until dad see's this, he's not going to like it one bit. And Molly's right I don't want to stay here either.'

They all jumped with shock a moment later when they heard a loud crashing noise.

Molly and Oliver stared at their mother. 'Wait here, I mean it.' Fiona said as she rushed through into the kitchen, obviously they had disturbed whoever had been squatting here when they had come in.

Reaching the kitchen window she looked through and saw a tall youth in a black hoodie with fair tufts of hair sticking out of the sides, climbing over the back fence. If not for the fact that he had caught his black jeans on a nail, Fiona guessed that he would already have been gone. She breathed evenly a moment later, as with a giant heave of his left leg he tore himself free of the fence and quickly disappeared over the top.

About to yell at him, she suddenly stopped herself, she had no idea of how many had been in the house; could have been a dozen or more squatting, judging by the mess. And if the last one out saw a lone woman, however many there were out there in a split second they could all come pouring back into the house, and do God only knows what.

The back yard was littered with rubbish which had fallen from the bin that he must have knocked over in his rush to escape. She gripped the edge of the sink, her knuckles going white then regretting it when she felt something sticky, glancing down into the sink she saw day's old vomit and realised that was the source of one of the many smells.

'Oh how disgusting.' Gagging, she turned and looked for something to wipe her hands with. There was nothing in the filthy kitchen that she trusted to wipe her shoes on never mind her hands. She turned the hot tap on and let the water run over her hands, after a few minutes when the steam was rising into her face, and the mess in the sink was finally gone, she wiped her hands on the back of her cream trousers, and with a quick shudder marched back into the sitting room where her children were sitting on the edge of the ripped settee, both of them staring at her and both with same look of disgust on their faces.

'Okay. I'm not having this, never mind your father.' She pulled her mobile phone out and stabbed at the numbers, in a moment it was answered. 'What the hell do you think you're playing at?' She yelled.

'What...What do you mean?' the deep male voice on the other end asked.

Fiona proceeded to tell him just exactly what she meant. When she finally ran out of steam he quickly replied. 'Okay, I'm sorry it should have been examined...I actually thought it had. In fact I'm sure it was seen and passed the day before yesterday, that's why I let you go on alone, much better than having anything that resembles a police escort...I'll see what I can do and then I'll pick you up in half an hour, just keep calm... And stop worrying, it will be alright. I'll meet you beside the monument in Grainger Street. Grab a taxi I'll reimburse you.'

'You just fucking bet you will.' She replied, snapping her phone shut.

'Come on. We're getting out of here now.' She snatched her bag up.

Blissfully unaware of what was going on and why they had left their home in Gosforth in such a hurry, her children, frowning at each other in a mixture of puzzlement and awe that their own mother had sworn on the phone, they silently followed her out of the house.

Twenty minutes later they were standing outside of Greys monument in Newcastle city centre. Fiona had bought some sweets to keep the kids quiet, the rare treat certainly worked on Molly, though not so much on Oliver, who looked at the packet of fruit gums with distain, as they went and sat on the steps and stared at the man preaching to the early morning crowds, who intent on their own business mostly ignored him and passed on by, as his three helpers handed brightly coloured leaflets out.

Across the road on the corner of the street next to Waterstones bookshop, a thin young man wearing a black t-shirt and skinny black jeans which hung way low at the back, and made him look even thinner than he was, and with long unkempt fair hair and dark sunglasses that he kept pushing back up his nose, he set up a box for donations, then slinging his guitar strap over his shoulder, he started strumming his guitar and in a passable voice started singing, *The Road To Hell.*

And that's what I'm on alright. Fiona was thinking, as the young man received glaring looks from the preacher just as Fiona spotted the man she was waiting for, as with phone stuck to his ear, and with the look on his face which made Fiona guess he was giving someone a hard time.

As long as it's about me and the dump they sent me to, and

where is Stella, she said she would be here? She thought, as the man hurried towards her.

DS Jerry Steel, tall fair haired and suntanned from a recent holiday in Italy, and a strong liking for beige coloured suits, that would look more at home on a retired London business man than a DS from the Northeast, reached Fiona, she could tell by his dark brown eyes, unusual with his colouring, that he seemed genuinely sorry for this mess.

'That should never have happened Fiona,' he said quickly, shoving his phone in his pocket. 'I really can't apologise enough. Trust me whoever is responsible will be sorted…I honestly thought it had been checked over again this morning. Trust me I wouldn't have sent you otherwise. And DI Stella Hawkes sends her apologies; she says she will get through to see you in a day or two.'

'Hmm.'

He looked warily at her, seeing her disappointment that DI Hawkes wasn't here, and knowing that he might have misjudged her, at first thinking that where she came from she was probably the type to look down her nose at him and most of the world. But he might have been wrong, she was, although a bit snobby at times, far from being the stuck up bitch he'd first thought. Although, he reasoned with himself, the jury's still out on that, his wife did say quite often that he was a terrible judge of character.

Fiona, never frightened to say her piece at the best of times, could also be very reasonable when she'd calmed down. This however was not one of those times. 'Right-so what the hell do we do now?' She snapped, looking down at Oliver and Molly, then back at DS Steele. With a, don't you dare give me fucking bull shit look on her face.

With nearly closed lips DI Steele ran his tongue around his mouth, something he was always doing which had seriously grated on Fiona's nerves this past week, and she was getting very, very close to telling him. Instead she held her peace, took a deep breath and waited to hear what he said next.

'I've spoken to a rather good colleague of mine.' he nodded his head and smiled as if he'd just done something wonderful. 'DI Lorraine Hunt, from Houghton Le Spring. A small town between Sunderland and Durham; nice place- ever been there before?'

Fiona shook her head, tired and sick to death of running, hiding and very nearly at the end of her tether, and nervously wondering where her husband was and his brother, both were supposed to contact her this morning and had not. Even though she had rung them both countless times, and at this moment she couldn't care less where the hell Houghton Le Spring was. It could be on the other side of the moon for all she cared. All she wanted was a safe haven for her family. And to be by the side of her oldest son's bed...And for all of this, this terribly frightening nightmare they had found themselves in, to be well and truly over. Her children deserved better than this.

'Okay, you err- you're sure you weren't followed? 'He glanced around as he spoke. 'You did keep checking like I said- Didn't you? Because it is very important.'

Oliver's eyes narrowed when he heard this. He quickly glanced from the man in front of him to his mother. He couldn't make sense of what was happening, but he knew something was wrong, he just wished his mother would tell him. All this rubbish about holidays in other people homes, she thinks I'm six. And Dad's as bad, where's he at?

'Not that I'm aware of.' Fiona glared at Steel, her eyes boring into him, before flicking towards her children.

Shit, he thought, fairly put me foot in it there. He glanced at Oliver, who was watching him with narrowed eyes, then quickly back at Fiona. He knew that she was a woman on the edge, her whole life thrown in to chaos, through no fault of her own or her family, and that all she wanted was to be back in last week when life was uncomplicated, and instead she was standing here, the very last place she wanted to be.

'DI Hunt is sending someone to meet us in the next half hour or so. Please follow me.' He picked one of Fiona's bags up, looked around and frowned when he saw a very tall thin man with a long grey beard staring at them, the man stared back for a moment then turned and walked away.

'Who was that?' Fiona asked, her heart beginning to thump.

'It's fine. Nothing to worry about,' Steel smiled, showing large white teeth, 'friendly, if he'd turned the other way...'

'If he'd turned the other way...What?'

'Nothing,' realising he'd said too much, Steel looked around again, then nodding and smiling at Fiona, he said. 'Come on then, we best get moving.' He turned left towards the car parks at the Newcastle football ground.

With a sigh, Fiona picked up her bags yet again, guessing rightly that the bearded man had been watching over them, and pleased that they had, had some sort of protection, like the police had promised, looked down at her children and motioned with her head for them to follow, both of the children rose from the steps below the monument and flanking their mother, followed DS Steele to his car.

'But you said we could go in the bookshop...You promised me a new book.' Molly said.

'The shop isn't open yet and there isn't time to wait Molly. Besides you still have books I bought you the other day, unread.'

Molly gave a huge exaggerated sigh, stuck her bottom lip out and with a stamp of her foot, followed her brother.

God bless them, Fiona thought, they are innocents in all of this, why, why did you have to get us involved John and turn our lives upside down…And where the hell are you?

And where the hell are you Martin?

## CHAPTER FIVE

Whistling *Rule Britannia*, his favourite song, loudly and totally out of tune, which he always was although never to his ears, it never even occurred to him that he was the reason people went outside for a ciggie they didn't even want when it was his turn to sing at the karaoke nights.

Mr Jansen fastened the last button on his white shop coat, turned his collar down and smoothed his hair back, unlocking the shop door he peeped outside.

'Deserted.' he muttered disappointedly, a moment later though, his usual sunny nature took over as he went on. 'But it is Sunday morning, plenty of time. Come on you lovely people, shopkeepers have bills too.'

He took the newspaper board and stood it outside in the still deserted street, reread the latest headlines with his hands on his hips, shook his head vigorously at the state of the world, and tutted, before going back inside his shop. His head still shaking he walked up the bread and biscuit isle, tucking things in and snaffling a packet of custard crèmes as he passed.

'I swear the bloody world's getting worse every day. Full of drug crazed idiots, and that's just the friggin daft do- gooders, never mind the rest of the nutters.'

After crunching on three custard crèmes and debating whether or not to have another, he rubbed his increasing waistline and decided against it, he really needed to do some stock taking. If only to shut her upstairs up for a few hours, he reached for a clip board and started on the canned goods isle. He'd hardly whistled his way through the first chorus of his next favourite, *'Oh What A Beautiful Morning,'* and was counting the tins of peas, when he heard the bell ring on top of the shop door.

'Oh oh, first customer of the day at last,' he muttered with a smile. 'And about time an 'all.' He rubbed his hands together.

He so hated stock taking, and would rather have a shop full of customers or a hole in his head, anything rather than the dreaded stock take. But life was much better when she who must be obeyed, was happy.

He peeped round the corner of the isle and drew a quick harsh breath. With narrowed eyes he watched the youth walk in and pick a pint of milk out of the fridge...And swallowed hard. Quickly he made his way back to the counter.

It is him, he thought, the horrible lousy bastard, his heart started to sink, as the youth, glaring defiantly at him swaggered down the aisle towards him.

Swallowing hard again, Mr Jansen began tidying the counter. Thinking as he stacked packets of sweets on top of the packets of sherbet, Dev that's his name.

The horrible bastard who threatened to torch my shop.

How bloody well dare he?

Thought he'd gone forever when Jacko gave him a good beating for what he did to his Melanie, threatening the poor bairn with a knife. The twat got everything he deserved.

Well I'm not frightened of the git.

No way, the stroppy bastard!

How fucking dare he, strutting about my shop like he's got nowt at all to worry about.

As if he owns the place, the cheeky horrible git. Oh if I was only a few years younger. I'd show him the road home on the end of me shoe alright, the prick.

How dare he even walk into my shop?

Kids these days- eh, he shook his head. No discipline, stupid do-gooders, it's all their flaming fault. Ruination of the country and by the time people wake up, it'll be too bloody late.

Reaching the counter Dev stared at the shopkeeper who refused to meet his eyes, after a silent moment he threw a pound coin on the counter, which rolled along then skidded onto the floor

'Keep the change mate.' He said with a sneer, as he turned and slowly walked away.

With shaking hands the shopkeeper bent down and picked the coin up. As he slowly rose he looked at the door which led to their living space upstairs, thanking God that his wife had not suddenly appeared.

He cursed himself for being frightened, once upon a time he would have shown a punk like him just where to go with a kick up the arse, but he was an old man now. And today he felt it.

'I guess it's time to retire.'

'Nice little house up the lovely Whitley bay area. Right on the coast, to be able to sit there on a morning and watch the sun come up-heaven.'

It's what they had always talked about doing, whenever the time came. Sadly he looked around the shop he had owned for the last forty years. With his hands still trembling and a tear forming in the corner of his eye he opened the till drawer and dropped the money in, then eyes wide in fear, he clutched at his chest as a sudden harsh pain engulfed him.

## CHAPTER SIX

He was tall dark haired and handsome, with deep brown eyes, dressed in a pale blue T-shirt and wearing a pair of dark blue shorts that showed his mussel bound legs off as he strode along the beach. He had spotted the girl sitting alone on the beach, some fifty yards away; he hovered for a while to make sure that she was alone, before moving in.

She was sitting on the sand with her knees pulled up to her chin, her arms wrapped around her legs staring out to sea. He eyed the girl up as he walked towards her, just about right he thought. Blonde, though it looks like it's out of a bottle, not that it matters. She's about sixteen maybe eighteen tops.

'Perfect.' He muttered.

He looked around, the beech was still deserted. He whistled loudly and his dog, a gentle, "everybody's friend golden retriever" named Sally ran towards him her tail wagging furiously.

He'd glanced quickly at the girl and saw her head turn towards him, then look at the dog. Without obviously looking at the girl he made a fuss of Sally, then headed in the girls direction. When he reached her he pretended to be startled at nearly bumping into her. Apologising, he quickly hid a smile when she just laughed and immediately started making a fuss of Sally, who tried to return every pat with a kiss.

A little more than ten minutes later, the man knew all about the girl's own dogs, two Boxers, Bertie and Bill, and also where she lived, which school she attended, for his first guess had been right, she was only sixteen. Or so she said.

'So,' he glanced along at the ice cream van. 'You want strawberry or vanilla?'

'Strawberry please....With sprinkles,' she batted her heavily made up eyelashes at him, as standing up and smiling, she took the dog's leader from his hand.

Within the space of twenty minutes he'd found out that her name was Sarah Rose Sinclaire, and that she had fallen out with her parents, because she was sick of being treat like a child. Both parents worked with a baby brother in day care, and if she wasn't in the house when they came in there was hell to pay, and since the baby brother had arrived they treat her like a slave.

Her best friend, who she had been friends with since the very first day of school and her boyfriend of six months had also pissed her off when she'd caught them snogging last night behind the garages where she lived

'Can you believe it?' She said shaking her head.

Nodding his agreement with her, he suggested they take a walk further along the beach.

'Oh yes.' She said eagerly.

Sarah Rose Sinclaire was in love.

He grabbed her hand as Sally made a sudden lunge for the water and dragged the girl who was still holding her leader, forward.

'So, won't they be looking for you?' He asked, a few minutes later, still holding her hand. 'The family?'

'I'm not a bit kid you know,' she replied, smiling coyly up at him. 'Besides, they're both at work today and won't be back till five.'

'In that case you might as well come to mine for lunch, like that would you?'

'Where is it?'

'Just up the road. My uncle owns a pizza shop.'

## CHAPTER SEVEN

PC Carter stared at the top of his mother's plump head, hoping, praying, the sixth sense she normally used to suss out what he was up to, would kick in sooner than later and that she would put her book down, knowing for a fact if he disturbed her latest Stephen King novel her heavily permed white hair, which was once bright ginger like his, would turn a very dark shade of purple to match her face, and she would probably kill him. What she would do when she found out what he had to tell her, he had no idea, except that she would probably kill him.

He moved his gaze to the kitchen window and watched a couple of black birds having a standoff with a grey pidgin over a crust of bread, and was startled a moment later when his mother spoke, his whole body jumped.

'Okay what is it?' she snapped. 'Come on I haven't got all bloody morning to waste.'

'Mam!'

'You've been staring at me for ages…Spit it out.'

'I, err…I've got something to tell you.'

She tutted. 'Obviously.'

Carter took a deep breath. 'Well it's like this mam, I err... I'm...I have to tell...' Before he could say anymore his mobile rang, looking apologetically at her, he rose from his chair and walked to the window.

'Yes boss?' He spent the next few minutes nodding his head and avoiding eye contact with his mother.

When he put his phone away his mother said. 'Well, come on spit it out.'

'What?'

'You had something to tell me.'

'I...' Quickly he put his uniform jacket on. 'Sorry mother, that was the boss, 'I've got to go...I'll tell you...I'll tell you about it tonight. Okay.'

'Yeah right. Course you will.'

Quickly slapping his pockets to check that he had everything, and knowing his mother was now staring stubbornly at him, he refused to meet her eyes. 'Bye. See you tonight,' he muttered quickly as he hurried out of the room.

His mother slowly shook her head at his retreating back, and mumbled to herself, 'Bet you do.' before going back to her book.

Outside Carters mobile rang again, taking the call as he walked to his car which was at the end of the street because some neighbour's friends had parked in his space last night, and when they had finally up and gone, he was far too tired to go out and move it.

After saying four times, 'Yes boss.' He quickly put his phone in his pocket.

He did a sharp turnaround. Reached home and ran up the eight stone steps to the Victorian house which had been in his family from the day it was built.

'It's only me,' he called, as he took the stairs two at a time. 'Police business.'

'Well who the flaming hell else, or what else, would it be? Unless the fantastic Mr Dean Martin decided to pay me a visit.' His mother said, without taking her eyes off her book.

Who the flaming hell's Dean Martin? He thought, reaching his bedroom.


Five minutes later, having changed into a dark grey suit, and white shirt which he left open at the neck, he popped his head round the corner of the door. 'Police business mam, had to change into civvies. Sort of undercover, you know, so the locals won't know I'm a copper like.'

'Really! Never would have guessed.'

'Yes. It's a very important job,' he stuck his chest out, 'they don't give jobs like this to just any old copper...Just the one's they know who can do it.'

'Okay son, err…Wasn't there something you wanted to tell me? The books finished now.'

'Not much time...'

'But I'm all ears now,' she patted the seat next to her. 'Come on son, talk to your mam.'

He turned towards the outside door 'Laters mam.'

'Hmm... Now I just wonder what it is you want to tell me?'


Fifteen minutes later Carter was waiting outside of the library in Houghton Le Spring where he'd been told to meet Fiona, her children, and DI Steel, to hand the keys to a safe house over. He looked to the right along the street and spotted a traffic warden giving his car a good looking over.

'No'...Yelling at the top of his voice he ran along to him. 'Hey, you can't do that. No way.'

'Sorry sir, but I can.'

'But that's my car. You can't give me a ticket.'

'Just watch me mate, you're illegally parked in a disabled bay without a badge.' The traffic warden, overweight and red faced, stared at Carter.

'Now look here, I've already said you can't do that.'

'And why would that be?'

'I'm a police officer on official duty.' Carter blustered. 'You are not allowed to impede the law in their duties.'

'Yeah, like that hasn't been tried before.' The traffic warden laughed, then carried on writing the ticket and slapped it on the car window.

'It's true.' Carter rummaged in his pockets for his badge, then with a sinking feeling he realised he'd left it at home in his uniform. 'Shit!'

'No need to be abusive, else I'll call the real coppers. You can get into real trouble for impersonating the police.'

Carter shook his head, turning he looked back at the library and saw DS Steel standing next to a very angry looking woman with a couple of obviously bemused kids in tow, he guessed this was the woman he was supposed to meet.

'Just wait here I'll only be a minute. Don't go.' He threw over his shoulder at the traffic warden, as he quickly ran back to the library entrance, very nearly decapitating an old man who was about to sit at a table outside of the café next to the library, as he rushed passed him.

'Hello I'm PC Carter,' he said quickly with a smile, when he reached Fiona and DS Steel. Looking at DS Steel who he had met twice before, he said. 'Nice tan.'

'A week in Italy, do it every time.' Steel pruned himself, as Fiona turned and glared at him.

'You're ginger!' Molly said. Then putting her hand over her mouth she started to giggle with her brother.

'Molly.' Fiona turned her glare on her daughter.

Carter smiled at the girl, thinking, you're only a few shades from ginger yourself, little monkey.

After a moments awkward silence, DS Steel introduced them. Carter shook a very stiff hand belonging to the woman Steel introduced as Fiona Smith, and looking more than pleased to be rid of them all, Steel flashed his teeth, said a quick goodbye, before hurrying off.

'Whoa, hang on,' Carter said. 'I'm only supposed to hand the keys over.'

'There's been a change of plan. I'm needed back in Newcastle ASAP. Something urgents come up...Sorry gotta rush.'

'But!' Fiona looked at him.

Steel shrugged as he hurried away. 'Sorry, there's nothing more I can do. You're in Houghton le springs hands now.'

'Charming.' Fiona said.

Turning quickly round to face his car, Carter frowned when he noticed that the traffic warden had disappeared. He strained his neck to try and see his windshield, and then smiled with relief when it looked free of any ticket.

He must have had a change of heart, he thought.

His smile dropped a minute later though, as they walked towards the car and he saw the ticket still attached to the bottom of his car window. 'Damn.' he muttered, knowing that it was no one's fault but his own for leaving his badge in his uniform jacket.

He quickly snatched the ticket off the window and stuffed it in to his pocket. Hoping that the woman with him hadn't noticed, and wondering if he should give it to Lorraine or Luke to sort, after all he was an undercover officer on duty. He puffed his chest out.

Best give it to Luke, he thought. More chance of catching him on his own. And the boss was pretty occupied with things at the moment, she just might forget about it.

Because if Dinwall finds out I'll never hear the last of it!

He'll take the piss forever.

Opening the car door, he ushered Fiona inside, then opened the back door for the children. He couldn't help himself, he just had to pull a face at the little girl when she pointed to his head and giggled again. Her brother tried to hide a grin and shaking his head looked out of the window.

A few minutes later they pulled up outside of an empty house on the Seahills estate. Carter opened the car door for Fiona and her family and moved them quickly up the path and into the house. In their hurry and her anxiety to see inside, Fiona did however notice the freshly mowed lawns on either side of the path, and the spring flowers in full bloom. That's something I suppose, she thought. It might not be as bad as the last one.

Fingers crossed. Please don't let it be anywhere like the last...The last...Shit hole.

'Hmm,' she said, pleasantly surprised once they were inside the house and she was looking around, 'I suppose it's a lot better than the last flaming dump, at least its tidy. And the furniture looks safe to sit on...'

'It doesn't stink either.' Molly wrinkled her nose, as Oliver ran up stairs. 'Not like the last house-cos that was a fucking disgrace wasn't it mum.'

'Molly!' Fiona was mortified.

'But that's what you said...Didn't you mum?' Molly looked up at her mother.

Fiona was saved from answering by Oliver. 'Yeah, it's got three bedrooms,' he shouted from the top of the landing. 'Not a very big bathroom, though mum, just a bath and toilet and it's shared, but there's no shower.'

'Well at least it's a bedroom each.' Fiona replied. Her face still red, she turned to Carter who was trying not to grin.

'Yes...'

But that was as far as he got as she quickly went on. 'So what sort of estate is this then, a drug haven or what?' she demanded, in an attempt to hide her embarrassment. 'And, any known pedos…I need to protect my children from?' She glared at Carter as she moved to the window then turning to look out she watched as a small girl from the house opposite walked down her path, crossed the road, and stared at her from the pavement.

'No…It…' Carter felt like a small child in the head masters study being blamed for something he didn't do. 'Well, like most council estates it has a few problems,' he hesitated for a moment then went on with a smile. 'But the majority are good decent hard working people…Until the court case you and the family should be alright here, very nice and neighbourly people.' Carter nodded his head thinking as he did so; actually most of the really big bad guys come from your sort of posh place.

'Would you live here?'

'Hmm…' He smiled, thought for a moment then nodding again said. 'Actually, yes I would.'

She looked at him, and then finally shrugging said. 'Okay…If you say so…It's not like we really have much choice do we?' She snapped.

Carter started to back pedal out of the room. 'I'll leave you then, you have the numbers if you need us. Remember we're only on the other end of the phone, also undercover patrols will be around often, day and night...Oh, and both of the schools are sorted...Alright?'

'School!' Molly pulled a face behind her mother's back, as she quietly muttered. 'Another dump, really mum, this is not fun. I don't like it.'

'Yes thank you.' With a quiet sigh, Fiona closed the door behind Carter, not having heard what Molly had said and not realising that her daughter was standing right beside her until she pulled at her jacket.

Turning Fiona looked down at her, a questioning look on her face. 'Mum, you're not listening to me, when are we going home, cos I think this is a stupid silly holiday, just trying other people's houses out? Horrible houses, with horrible people.'

'Molly!'

'And none of them have a swimming pool, do they...? I want to go home...I want to see aunt Olivia...I want my dad...I want to go home... And, and what's a... a court case?'

'Oh darling, it's fun, don't you think. You'll make lots of new friends at your new school...Wont you. It's like a sort of student exchange isn't it...You know what, in a few years you will be able to exchange with French students.' Fiona babbled, hoping to throw Molly's question about the court case off. Trying other people's homes out as a sort of holiday was the only thing she had been able to come up with to tell them, selling it as a sort of adventure, though she guessed Oliver wasn't buying it. And all Molly had done was complain.

'But I want my own things and my room, and my own friends...Camilla will be looking for me I've never seen her for ages...Don't like it here.' She stamped her foot. 'Really mum it...it's an awful dreadful place, the kind of place you say we should never go to.'

'Now you haven't given it a chance Molly. Anyhow,' Fiona pointed out of the window, 'she looks...Well, she might be a nice little girl.' She looked at the small girl across the road who was still staring in the window.

Molly folded her arms, her face taking on her mother's own stubborn look. 'Her...' she pointed at the girl across the road. 'It's rude to stare in people's window's that's what you say... Don't like it here.' She stamped her foot again. 'Really want to go home. I want my own friends, not that scruffy thing out there. She doesn't know what a bath is, and she's ugly...Bet the schools full of uglies just like her...I want to go home...' Molly stared defiantly at her mother. 'I heard you talking to aunt Olivia, the other day, and she said these people were the big,' she thought for a moment, 'the great unwashed. Didn't she?'

Fiona frowned, her daughter was starting to sound very much like her sister in law Olivia, who as Molly had picked up on, had no time for what she called the great unwashed. 'Heathens,' was her favourite saying. She looked down at Molly, half expecting her to come out with the word.

'Molly, that's unkind.'

Molly shrugged. 'But you didn't say that to aunt Olivia, did you mum?'

In the doorway Oliver was standing watching them. He too wanted to go home, hated all this jotting from house to house, and as his mother had guessed he also knew this was not a holiday. He'd heard the constant rows over the last week, the loud whispers they thought he couldn't hear between his mum and dad and his uncle; he was old enough to know that they were frightened of something, all of them, even his dad who wasn't frightened of any one. And that fact made him frightened, even more than the fact that his brother was in the hospital fighting for his life.

Wonder if the accident really was an accident?

He pictured his brother Liam, his face as white as the sheets on the hospital bed with tubes and wire's all over him, and felt frightened all over again. Wishing that whatever this was all about would be gone, whatever his father, uncle and mother had seen that day had never happened.

He knew more than his parents thought he did, he also, although he and his sister had never talked about it, guessed that Molly knew more than she was letting on. And if his mother stopped treating her like a baby she also would know that Molly was more aware than she thought.

Unaware that her son was watching her, Fiona stared at Molly. Oh how she herself wanted to go home. And how the hell do you explain to kids that there was no way that they could, their large beautiful house with two acres of gardens and a swimming pool, just wasn't safe anymore, and may never be, already she had given the police a list of their most valuable possessions, these by now should be safe in storage.

After a moment she took her mobile out and checked for missed calls, none. In a way she was relived, it meant that the hospital had not called her with bad news about Liam, thank God. Her oldest son was a fighter she kept telling herself over and over, he would pull through.

'He will.' She muttered.

Liam has his whole life in front of him. He's determined he wants to be a doctor.

'And he will...He will.'

Her brother in law though, should have phoned over an hour ago, that had been the plan in case anything went wrong and her husband couldn't phone, frowning her frustration she moved to the bottom of the stairs, passing Oliver who had not moved from the doorway. Fiona glanced at him then quickly looked away, knowing that he definitely suspected something. Perhaps Oliver hasn't quite got the brains to be a doctor like his brother, but he's far from stupid.

But she couldn't tell them what had happened. No way must they know what they had seen that night.

She felt like stamping her foot the way that Molly often did, then a stray thought took her out of her private terror for the moment, as a picture of Molly having one of her usual hissy fits entered her mind.

Fiona cringed. She's a spoilt brat!

Why have I never realised this before?

Am I a bad mother?

To busy with other things?

She felt like crying, this on top of everything else.

Then as always the memory of their plight chased everything else away. Things had changed forever, so much that even after the court case was over they had been advised to move as far away as possible. John had already checked out a few properties in different countries, none of which she liked. Because this was home, this is where she wanted to bring up her children, live her life.

She sighed. In England.

Where they were born.

Why, through no fault of their own should they have to move?

It just wasn't fair.

She took a deep breath, and tried hard to stop her heart from fluttering as she took out her phone and dialled the hospital to check that there really was no bad news about her oldest son.

## CHAPTER EIGHT

Mrs Archer left the hotel she owned under one of her many pseudonyms, in a secluded street in the seaside town of South Shields. The hotel was a front for prostitution and one of her many earners; after instructing the driver to take her home to Houghton Le Spring via the coast road. She got in to the back of the navy blue limousine with gold trimmings, and relaxed for a moment; with a tight smile and a contented sigh from her heavily botoxed lips, she patted the leather seat.

'Mine all mine.' She whispered to herself.

This last couple of years not one, but all of her sidelines had really paid off big time, more than she had ever dreamed possible. The girl from the wrong side of the tracks has fairly hit the big time. She grinned to herself. In fact it's high time I drove down the old neighbourhood, I'm sure aunt Mary is still alive, even though the old goat hates my guts.

She grinned again. One day next week. Just to let her know how well I've done. The grin turned into a high pitched laugh, as the driver nervously looked at her through his mirror.

She nodded to herself, well, perhaps after my holiday. I've got more than enough to pay another visit to Switzerland, every year for ever. She rather fancied some breast implants this time. Nothing like a pair of nice firm boobs. Perhaps a little bit of a tummy tuck.

She would also not be flying this time, but going in the fabulous yacht she had just acquired. Once she got a decent crew sorted that was. It was finding some trustworthy low life's, the three she'd interviewed so far, just didn't cut it. There was however an old friend of hers who was back on the scene after spending a few years at her Majesty's pleasure, he should do.

A few weeks time, she thought, when the weather warms up properly. So I can just sit back and relax for a change. From what she'd seen this morning, a few of her main ventures were in very good hands.

Suddenly she sat up straight just as they were entering Tynemouth, and gave the driver a different set of directions, he quickly took a right, and a few minutes later they pulled up outside of a large building in one of the side streets on the opposite side of town. A sign on the front said Pizza To Go Now. Already there was a line of hungry people forming outside.

Been quite a while since I paid a drop in visit to this lot, she thought, as she put one silk stockinged leg after the other out of the car. Standing, she threw the ends of her purple silk scarf over her shoulders, pulled her light brown fur coat a little tighter and walked over to the door. The coat was mink, Mrs Archer had no love for humans and she certainly didn't care about which animal had lost its life to keep her warm. She had an assortment of animal furs, and loved them all. Especially the ones she had shot herself.

To Mrs Archer there was nothing like the thrill of the hunt, be it animal or human. Reaching for the handle on the glass door, and not missing the look of pure shock on the small dark haired man's face, who was standing behind the counter, before he turned and ran into the back room. It took her four strides to reach the counter and then she was lifting the flap on the side, and following him through.

Her way was suddenly blocked by a taller much younger man, wearing a blue t-shirt and shorts, who was very handsome indeed, she couldn't help thinking, as he lifted his arm up to stop her. In a threatening voice, which sounded vaguely German, he said, 'Stop, you can't go through there, it's private. Out now woman...Go...Go now.' As he stepped forward with a menacing look on his face, he lifted his arms palms out, as if to push her back.

She stared into his eyes. 'If you value your hands you will fucking put them down...Now....Right now.'

For a moment he was startled, no woman- and very few men,

had ever spoken to him like this before. He stared at her, his eyes narrow slits, but far from being intimidated, she took another step forward. He started to retreat as she relentlessly without once dropping her eyes kept on moving towards him. When her toes were touching his, he said. 'But.'

'But- I own the fucking place, knob head.'

'I...Do you?'

'Fucking move.'

When he still stood there staring at her she screamed, 'Now! Fucking wanker.'

'It's alright Arnulf,' another man, English this time, small in stature, with a thick dark beard stepped between them. With a tight smile he ushered Mrs Archer through into the back room, as Arnulf did a quick disappearing act down the corridor, and stripping off his blue t-shirt got back to work.

'I don't understand,' the small man said after offering her a seat. 'I thought we sorted the business last night. The monthly money was exact. As it always is... Right to the last penny.' He stuttered slightly as he went on. 'Please would you like some refreshment? We can get you anything you want, anything at all. If it's not on the premises, that's not a problem. I can have it here in five minutes.'

'No... And, yes as usual the money was exact, that's according to my accountant.'

She eyed him up and down, noting that although a tad nervous that she had arrived without telling him, he certainly did not look as if he had anything to hide. He had worked for her a long time now, and she'd never had reason to doubt him, in fact she had found him more than loyal, he would do anything he could to keep in her favour... Anything.

'I thought it was about time I gave the place a look over, it's been a while since I paid you a visit...And who the fuck is that moron?'

'Certainly, that's up to you, and that moron is Arnulf, only been here about a month or so arrived off a boat from Germany and came highly recommended, a damn good worker. And- he and his dog, lovely Golden Retriever, just brought a fine piece of merchandise in.'

'Good. Looks strong enough.'

'Stamina of a bull- you know what I mean. He just keeps on going.' He grinned at her, as he gestured for her to follow him.

They went through the door into a badly lit room which was obviously used by the cooking staff through the day, and was decorated in various shades of brown which made it look even more dingy than it really was. Three men were playing cards at a table by the window all of them knew her and all three kept their heads down, as they passed through into a much more opulent room.

Half an hour later, with the sound of a baby's cry in her ears and another happy grin on her face, she stepped back into the Limo.

## CHAPTER NINE

Lorraine, sick of watching the telly and the constant stream of bad news, had decided to go for an early drive to pass the time before work. But work had caught up with her via a phone call from DI Steel. Now an hour later and hoping that Carter had done the job thoroughly, she was sitting on a bench at Roker beach staring out at the now calm sea. A small yacht was slowly moving along the horizon, its white sails shining bright against the blue sky and even deeper blue sea.

She looked up at the clear sky with a slight smile on her face; now that the rain clouds had finally disappeared, it looked like a very promising start to the day. The sun, although not hot was nice and warm for this time in the year. You could smell and taste the salt in the air- the smell of the sea always invigorated her, and she loved being this close to the shore.

Taking a last sip from her can of diet coke she placed the empty can at her side, standing it next to her favourite chocolate bar wrapper. With both hands she gripped the edge of the bench and leaned forward as if she needed that extra push to help her stand up. But no, physically Lorraine was very fit, her problem lay elsewhere.

She hadn't planned on staying this long, even though her first shift back after a long break, which she hadn't wanted, didn't start till eleven, but her dog Duke was enjoying the beach and the odd paddle which was as far in the water as he would go, if you could call it a paddle seeing as he barely got his paws wet. Duke of doubtful parentage, but with definitely German, shepherd, retriever and some collie in the mix. Tan and black in colour, adored his mistress.

"Well he's definitely not a bloody swimmer then." Lorraine remembered her mother Mavis, saying six years ago, when as a frisky five month old puppy, they had first brought Duke to the beach and all he had done was stare at the water for a few moments before turning and making a sudden bolt for the car, causing other dog owners to laugh, as they passed. She sighed, as she pushed her long blonde hair off her shoulder, pulling a thin brown hair band off her wrist, she tied her hair back into a pony tail, then glanced down at her new silver watch, a recent present from Luke. For a moment her gaze lingered on the watch; then she shook herself.

Really should be getting a move on, she thought, but she loved it here, had done since for as long as she could remember and she had actually been very surprised to find as many people as there were out so early, walking their dogs or jogging, it actually seemed as if just about everybody in Sunderland had been out jogging in the rain earlier. There had been a couple of eager sandcastle builders too. The sandcastles neglected by their builders, were now about to be washed away by the incoming tide. How she wished the tide could wash over her dreams and bury them in the sand forever, only they weren't dreams, they were fucking nightmares.

The beach was mostly deserted now- the last people she had seen about half an hour ago, were a young couple with a golden retriever, walking off the beach hand in hand. She guessed that most of the people who had been here, had probably gone to work, those who had work on a Sunday of course, but now for the moment, now there was just her and her dog, a thousand noisy seagulls overhead, dive bombing and flying round and round in patterns she wondered if even they understood.

And her thoughts.

She sighed, and looked to her right.

Roker beach and the adjoining Seaburn beach, had changed a lot due to a recent modernisation, which when finally finished, she reckoned would make both beaches a match for any seaside towns in England, plus the actual beaches were first class and perfect for sunbathing, both beaches had huge stretches of beautiful golden sands. Although the part that was Roker, certainly had its fair share of pebbles which made it a heaven for pebble hunters, something she herself had loved to do as a child.

'Shit,' she muttered out loud. 'Time to move it. God only knows what's waiting at work for me.' Knowing there was only so much procrastinating she could do and to be on time, she really had to leave now.

The bench creaked as she stood up. She dusted sand from her black jeans and red jumper, stamped her feet to rid her trainers of sand then whistled at Duke, who was standing at the very edge of the water his right front leg waving in the air, and looking very much like he was daring himself to put a paw in the water.

His ears flicked back when he heard Lorraine whistle and spinning round he ran straight towards her. Picking the can and the wrapper up, she threw them into the bin just as Duke reached her. She patted his head, and then they headed across the road to the car park. Reaching the car and accepting a very wet dog kiss, Lorraine lifted the boot and took an old towel out to dust the sand off Duke's paws.

'Well that was a waste of time yet again.' She looked at Duke's dry paws and smiled as he jumped into the back of the car. He did love running on the sand though. Lorraine sighed, wondering yet again why people couldn't be more like dogs, just fur bundles of love; instead we murder each other and worse. Shaking her head and giving one last look towards the sea she took a deep breath and drove away.

Today was her first day back after a long leave, and even spending last week on the beautiful tranquil Holy island of Lindisfarne with Luke, her batteries were still not fully charged. The fact that she had been kidnapped a few months earlier and had, had to fight for her life was still uppermost in her mind, but she would get there.

She would!

Oh yes!

She stuck her chin out, not be long now and the evil bastard will get what he deserves.

But for now, it was time to get back to work and keep her mind occupied. And to prove to Clark that she was more than ready, she had been shocked when he had insisted that she take that much time off, but he had been adamant and had even flattered her by saying he wanted his best cop back in perfect condition, for Clark that had been high praise indeed.

And now I'm more than ready. The bastard won't keep me down. She told herself as she drove along the road. Not long now and I hope the twat gets locked up with a bunch of perverts, so he can never walk straight again.

Passing the sign that led to the National Glass centre she smiled at a recent memory. The Glass centre had a glass roof that you could walk on, and Luke, after much encouraging to get him there, had practically freaked out one day last year when they had visited and walked over the roof staring down inside the building. Although with Luke it had been more of a hop, skip and a jump. She drove on, her thoughts once again, as always turned back to her kidnapping.

The fear she had felt when her kidnapper had taken his clothes off and she was helplessly tied to the chair naked, was something she doubted she would ever forget.

But that's what he had intended to instil in her, fear. Because fear is a great immobiliser, and the bastard was a control freak and that's what he'd wanted, control over her. Thank God she had reacted differently.

She shook herself and yelled, 'No way you horrible bastard,' as she punched the steering wheel.

'No way are you going to bring me down.'

'You bastard.'

'I am not playing the victim.'

'No fucking way!'

'Twat...It's alright Duke.' She said quickly, a moment later after taking a few deep breaths; when, picking up his mistress's mood and becoming distressed, Duke whined and stood up. Even though she knew it was far from alright and the only time she would get some sort of closure would be when the case finally went to court, and the horrible, slimy, creepy, git, got his just deserts, which was thank God, only a few days away. She knew that the closer it got the more agitated she was becoming, which is why after her initial two weeks off, Clarke had insisted she must take another two.

Luke had been fantastic even though he had been bearing the brunt of it. She sighed. All she wanted was it over and done with and the bastard behind bars for life. That way she could be free of him and get her own life back.

'Lie down, good Duke.' She said over her shoulder.

'Lie down now...Good boy.'

Huffing to himself, Duke turned around twice before flopping to the floor, then with a giant sigh he rested his head on his front paws, before sitting up a moment later and staring out of the window. He thumped his tail as a small boy in the car behind waved at him.

She passed St Peters church, remembering visiting it on the same day as she and Luke visited the Glass centre. Luke had a thing about old churches he loved visiting them, and had been thrilled to find out that the first church had been there since 674

AD, although only the west wall and porch still survived of that time. He'd been even more ecstatic to find out that it had actually been raided by Vikings in 793 AD. She'd had to practically drag him away from the place.

She smiled again, remembering saying to Luke. 'Yeah really, okay Luke, whatever turns you on mate...And, you are so starting to sound like Carter!'

Once over the Wearmouth Bridge she turned right, carried on past the new shopping centre which was in the process of being built on the old Vaux site, then the old courthouse on her left. Finally out of the city and after nearly being rear ended by a fancy navy limo with gold trim, a quick glance at the passenger in the back seat had made her frown, knowing she'd seen that face before but just couldn't quite pin point where. And the car sped off too fast for her to catch the number plate.

At last she was finally free of most of the traffic, as she headed towards Houghton cut and was home within eighteen minutes, which would have been much quicker if she also hadn't hit every red light on the way.

She jumped out of the car, told Duke to 'Stay.' Then ran into the terraced house she now shared with Luke, quickly ditched the trainers, jumper and jeans, then changed into a light grey trouser suit with a white blouse. After applying her makeup, she ran the brush through her hair, and decided to tie it up in a bun. She checked the letter box on her way out, empty of everything except the gas and electric bills.

And they can wait until tomorrow, one more day won't hurt, anyhow who the hell opens bills on a weekend? She thought, quickly picking them out of the box and dropping them on the small hall table.

Back outside she got into her car and dropped Duke off at her mothers. Declining a cuppa from her God mother Peggy, who she knew would keep her talking all day, given half a chance, she ran up stairs to check on her mother Mavis, who was recovering from her third bout of flu over recent months.

'You alright mam?' she asked, poking her head around the corner of the door.

Mavis, a relic of the hippy years, was sitting up in bed, a crossword puzzle book by her side, her long fair hair hanging loose and her blue silk nightgown a perfect match for the bedspread, and curtains, smiled at Lorraine. 'Of course I am pet I'll be up and about before you know it... Anyhow, what about you?' She raised an eyebrow as she looked at her daughter.

'I'm fine mam, nothing to worry about.'

'You sure?'

'Of course, now stop worrying about me and just concentrate

on getting better...How's Madame Hitler looking after you?'

'Exactly!' Mavis rolled her eyes. 'She won't even let me out of this bloody bed. I'm certain the daft bugger's got a secret camera hidden up here'

'Good, cos that's where you're staying, until you're fully better this time, okay. As for the camera...I don't think so.'

Mavis pulled a face. 'Yeah, whatever.'

Lorraine laughed. 'Attitude Mother.'

'Tut tut!'

Still laughing, Lorraine headed back down the stairs, shouting goodbye, and waving at Peggy, she quickly left and made her way to the station.

## CHAPTER TEN

Around the time that Lorraine had passed the Glass centre, the receptionist Paula Barnsley who was in work early, shivered; it seemed as if the sun had been behind the clouds for ages, though when she'd entered the building five minutes ago after dropping her twin boys, Harry and Brennan off at her sister's house, the rain clouds had gone and the sky was a clear blue.

The clouds must be back and it must be gonna rain again; shit, she thought, with another shiver, which brought her grandmother to mind, one of her favourite sayings if someone shivered in front of her was, 'Someone's just walked over your grave.' And that, reminded Paula that she would have to pay her a visit in the next few days. Which in reality was always a delight, she just wished she had time to visit her more often than once or twice a week. But with the twins it was amazing she got time to go to work.

Looking across the room, her pretty face, framed with light brown curls, twisted into a frown, the sunlight was pouring in from the glass roof and spilling all over the room, except strangely, for her spot. Frowning she sat down and pulled her chair closer to her computer, put her blue cardigan over her shoulders, slipped her reading glasses on and logged in.

'Come on, come on,' she said to the machine, then tutted. 'I swear its getting slower every day.'

Frowning again she looked up, thinking perhaps a colony of seagulls had decided to do a mess all together and totally block out the sun.

'What the?' She muttered unable to think of any reason why the glass panel above her should suddenly turn red. Or, for that matter, why any of them would!

A moment later she screamed as she made out the features of a man and realised the red liquid which was running down the glass in tiny rivers-was blood.

## CHAPTER ELEVEN

Vanessa Lumsdon rubbed some warmth into her thin arms as she stared out of her sitting room window, she shivered and wondering if she could afford to put the heating on this early on a morning, seeing as the last bill had been the biggest she'd ever paid. Seems they just charge what they want these days, her friend Sandra had said, when the last bill had arrived. 'Another friggin estimate.' she had went on as she slapped the bill on the table. 'Lazy twats, remember when they used to read them every quarter, now they just send estimates out.'

Vanessa smiled at the memory then continuing to speak out loud, answered her previous thought. 'Better not, none of the kids are complaining its cold, plus the suns came out, it'll sharp warm things up, no point in wasting money seeing as winter is behind us.' She nodded to herself as she pulled her lemon jumper down over her black trousers, and straightened the collar of her white blouse.

For a moment she played with a strand of her recently dyed brown hair, and wondered briefly why it never turned out exactly the colour on the box. Or better, why the flaming shop lifters, useless sods that they were, never got the exact bloody colour she told them too. Excuses- always friggin excuses.

'Thick as pig's shit the whole bloody lot of them. And that Mary, friggin hell, she's got a face like a slapped fucking arse, if you even have the nerve to complain. She better get everything on the list I gave her for Saturday. Or she'll have a friggin slapped face, never mind her arse.'

She was about to turn away from the window when she caught the back of a woman and what looked like two kids, entering the house across the street. 'Hmm,' she practically pressed her nose up against the glass.

'Looks like some new neighbours, wonder why nobody seems to stay too long over there? Well, not since Mrs Jacobs died a couple of years ago, have they. Nice car, if it belongs to them, might be just a friend's though.'

A minute later Vanessa made her way back to the kitchen and her ironing board, just as her daughter Kerry, dressed in black top and tight black cycling shorts under her high Vis jacket came running down the stairs. Kerry's hair was dark and cropped short, her build was slim, and the size of her breasts compared to her younger blonde sister Claire, bugged her daily. She lived for her running and the thought of one day holding a trophy high above her head for Great Britain, was never far from her mind. In the half dozen or so races she'd entered so far she had won every one and her coach had very high hopes of her going international. And his hopes and plans were set for this year.

She felt a tingle of excitement as she always did when she thought of it. She sat on the bottom stair to fasten the laces on her trainers and said. 'You've been talking to yourself again mam? It's getting to be a habit mind you...And you can't blame it on the dog, cos we haven't got one.'

'Just wondering aloud that's all.'

'What about now?'

'Just those new folks across the road.'

'What folks? It's been empty for months... Talking to yourself and now seeing things, not good Mother.'

Vanessa tutted. 'I saw some real people going into the old Jacobs house you daft sod, not bloody ghosts, for God's sake. And I was only flaming well wondering how long they were gonna stay, that's all...Cos nobody seems to stay long over there do they? I mean, the last lot were only there for a few bloody weeks. And not very friendly either definitely kept themselves to themselves, didn't they?'

Kerry shrugged. 'A detective you're not mother...It takes a lot more than watching all those murder mysteries you thrive on, to become a copper you know,' she laughed. 'I can just see you and Sandra in uniform, patrolling the Seahills.'

'Funny bugger.'

'I'm off for a run see you in a bit.'

'Okay, but don't forget to order the invitations for our Robbie's birthday off that mate of yours, mind, because I want this to be special and nowt to go wrong. Not every day you're twenty one. And he is still giving you mate's rates, isn't he? Cos I did budget them in on the price he gave you...And believe it or not, friggin sausage rolls cost an arm and a leg these days. Even off the bloody lifters, cheeky gits.'

'Stop worrying mam, I already told you he will, they're probably printed already...And the whole thing, well, it'll be great. Just chill.'

'Hmm, say's you!'

'Look, just stop worrying like I already said, I'll drop a few quid in the pot when I get me pay okay.'

'Aw, thanks pet.'

Kerry stood up, did a few stretching exercises then slammed the door on her way out.

Vanessa jumped, and muttered. 'Bloody little witch...Slam the door why don't you.'

Then she smiled, remembering how not so long ago she would

have been so out of it that she wouldn't have even heard the door slam, and a party for her son would have been the last thing on her mind. She jumped again a moment later when there was a loud banging on the door, wondering who it was this early on a Sunday morning, she walked along the hallway opened the door to find three people, two young girls, wearing light cotton dresses with cream cardigans draped over their shoulders, with matching brown bobs, and an older white bearded man, in a tan coloured suit, holding leaflets and smiling at her.

'Oh God,' she groaned loudly. 'Thanks but no thanks.' She was about to close the door on their still smiling faces, when her friend Sandra Gilbride, wearing the largest pair of red high heel shoes in existence, came tottering up the path.

Knowing full well who they were, Sandra sidestepped around them. Totally ignoring them she pushed Vanessa inside and slammed the door behind her.

'Bloody daft brainwashed idiots,' she said, following Vanessa into the kitchen. 'Why can't they just get on with it and leave people alone. I mean what the hell do they all do for a living, if they've got time to go knocking on peoples doors.'

'The dole?'

'Hu, far too well dressed for that.'

'Yeah right...Well anyhow,' Vanessa laughed. 'We all know

why you don't like them. Remember...'

Sandra smiled. 'Aye, that day I'll never forget it but,' she shrugged, 'I had to know,' the smile turned to a grin. 'And you nearly had a heart attack.'

'Do you friggin well blame me, inviting the last lot into the house then demanding to know why seeing as you are a bastard you can't get into heaven...God their faces. Where the hell did you get that idea from anyhow.'

Sandra shrugged. 'The internet is a very valuable source of information. So they say.'

Vanessa shook her head and looked skywards. 'Load of rubbish. You should know better than to believe anything you read on there. Half the flaming stuff's made up. And as for that facebooky thing, neighbours airing their dirty linen, teenagers baring their body's, and then wondering why they get attacked, or slagged off.'

'Ha'way man, it's not all bad, just a few crazies trying to spoil it for everybody else...And anyhow serves them buggers at the door right, bothering people, they sharp left with their bloody tails between their legs, didn't they though?'

'Hmm, gotta be some good ones amongst them.'

'Might be!'

They both burst out laughing as Vanessa picked up her iron

and Sandra put the kettle on.

A few minutes later they were sitting down enjoying their tea when Vanessa told Sandra about the new neighbours.

Sandra stood and went over to the window. The blinds were closed on the house opposite. She turned back to Vanessa. 'So, did you actually see anyone go in there?'

'For God's sake, not you an 'all!'

'What?' Sandra raised her eyebrows.

'Nowt...Just saw the back of a woman and some kids, think there might have been someone else in front, a bloke, but not sure, didn't get a look at their faces though.'

'I wonder why no one ever seems to stop there very long? I mean it's a nice enough house isn't it, people are crying out for houses these days and that one stops empty for weeks, sometimes months at a time, weird.'

'That's what I thought, but I've been thinking and I've just figured it out.'

'And?'

'It's because they see you tottering around on those high heels,' Vanessa laughed. 'Picture this mate, they're bloody frightened to death in case you fall on them and squash them to death, and they slide into the gutter never to be seen again.'

'Funny ha ha.' Sandra smiled, as she ran her long auburn plait through her fingers.

It was so good to see her friend happy; it had not always been so-far from it. Vanessa's life had been anything but easy, and most of it not even her own fault, apart from a few bad decisions, which anyone could make, and just when everything had at last seemed sorted and her alcoholism finally under control, her relationship with her kids good, and then the run up to Christmas had happened and what a run up, Sandra shuddered; the end of last year had not been good for either of them. But they had pulled together and pulled through, that was the main thing, the past was hopefully all wrapped up and behind them, and now, well now- was a new time.

She looked across at Vanessa, who as if reading her mind, reached over and patted her arm.

'It's good Sandra…All good.'

'You sure?'

'I am.'

Sandra put her arms around Vanessa and cuddled her. With tears in her eyes she said. 'We've come through the worst love, both of us, but especially you. But you know what, from now on it is gonna be really good…All good. As me mam Susan used to say. I can feel it in me bones.'

'Yes I remember her saying that. A bit spooky wasn't she, always talking like she knew weird things.'

'She was that. Anyhow from now on it's all forward, no looking back, ever.'

'Thanks to you.'

Sandra held her at arm's length and looked into her face. 'Please...Don't think I'll ever forget what you did for me all those years ago.'

'That's what friends are for...Do you ever think about...?' Vanessa looked into Sandra's eyes.

For a moment both of them were quiet, then Sandra dropped her gaze. 'I try not to.'

Vanessa hugged her. 'It was for the best love, different times back then.'

'I know,' she shuddered. 'Anyhow Robbie is going to have the best party ever.'

They hugged again and Vanessa wiped a tear from her eye. 'Thank you for being the best friend ever.'

'And you.'

## CHAPTER TWELVE

He was freezing and because he was shivering he knew he would be using up what little oxygen was left. He'd worried at the back of his mind for years about being buried alive after watching a film where the good guy was put in a coffin and left to rot.

More tears ran down his face.

I don't deserve this.

He punched the lid again and again. He knew he had split at least one of his knuckles, he could feel the blood running down his hands. But again he punched the lid.

For some reason he could feel no pain.

Has my body shut down to pain? He remembered when he was taking his driving lesson's, the abscess on his gum, which hurt like hell until he got behind the wheel, then the pain miraculously disappeared until he got out of the car and in moments was back again, when he'd asked a doctor friend why this was so, he had said that sometimes a high level of concentration on something could block out the pain.

Is that what is happening here?

How long?

How long have I been in here?

How long have I got left?

He tried to remember what he'd read about being buried alive, not much, something about five hours of oxygen if you are average size in an average size coffin.

How much less if you are tall in an average size coffin?

## CHAPTER THIRTEEN

Feeling happy, and on top form, Kerry was finding it hard to keep a grin off her face, because so much at home had changed lately, and finally at last for the better, and knowing her pace was really good this morning.

She was running past Lord Lambton's estate on the road down towards Chester Le Street, when she heard her phone. Slowing down she started jogging on the spot, pulled the phone out of her pocket and glanced at the screen. A moment later she stopped dead and eyes wide, stared at the message.

I'm watching you bitch.

'What!'

Not easily frightened, the message however did throw her; and for a brief moment her breath caught in her throat as she stared at her phone.

No way. She thought. She looked again, wondering if she'd been seeing things.

No, it was the same message. She shook her head, before quickly looking around. It was so quiet she could hear her heart pounding in her ears. The lack of any noise made everything seem a bit weird, or was it just her imagination getting the better of her?

She was alone, not a car on the road, nothing but the trees and across the road just down from the cottages, a field full of sheep, two or three of them were staring at her. Soon as if by telepathy most of the sheep had silently swung their heads towards her.

'Creepy or what?' she muttered. 'Getting a perv message like this is bad enough...Piss off sheep.'

She looked across the road towards the seven pink and cream painted cottages which stood at the junction towards Fencehouses and Houghton le spring, just as three cars passed her in quick succession.

Could someone be watching her from one of the houses?

Or were they in one of the cars?

Laughing their friggin heads off at me?

She heard a sound behind her and the hairs stood out on the back of her neck as a tingle of fear ran down her spine; fearing the worst, her body hyped up for fight or flight, she quickly spun round. A second later she blew air put of her cheeks then muttered. 'You stupid friggin idiot.' To the pheasant that was perched on top of the wall. Startled he took off back into the woods behind the wall where he had come from.

Who would send such a message? She wondered.

'Why?'

She took a deep breath just as her phone beeped again. She still had it in her hand and slowly, fearing the worst she looked at the screen.

You are one fucking dead bitch!

Her fear was replaced with anger; she resisted the temptation to throw her phone at the stone wall. Instead she switched it off and put it in her pocket, all the time looking around her.

Deciding that her best option was to go back home, she set off at a faster than normal pace.

## CHAPTER FOURTEEN

Having stopped off at a shop to replenish her stock of diet coke, Lorraine reached the police station the same time as Carter arrived. Closing her car door she took a deep breath, looked up at the building for a moment then pushing her shoulders back, she looked over at Carter as he got out of his car. 'All sorted with the incomers, Carter?'

'Yes boss.'

'Very good.'

'And welcome back boss, we've missed you.'

'Thanks Carter missed you too.' She smiled at him, and Carter blushed between his freckles.

She headed for the entrance and was on the top step before Carter caught up with her. A moment later they were both nearly knocked over, as three constables rushed out of the open double doors and headed down the steps, to one of the four parked up squad cars.

'Whoa where's the fire?' Lorraine asked, as she pressed herself up against the waist high wall.

'The Sunderland glass centre boss…Looks like there's been a murder.' PC Stevenson, tall and very slim, answered, as he followed the others to his squad car.

'What! You're kidding. I just passed there a half an hour ago, or less even. Everything looked alright to me…And Sunderland need our help, why?'

'Word is boss, nearly half the main stations down with some sort of a stomach bug.'

Lorraine raised her eyebrows, as Stevenson grinned. 'Probably one of the bad guys went in on purpose, determined to share. A sick joke, pardon the pun,' he grinned again. 'Oh and glad to see you back boss.'

'Thanks. And yeah to the bug…Like that hasn't been tried before,' she nodded. 'Okay, go…go.'

As Stevenson turned to go, DS Luke Daniels followed the constables down the steps. He paused for a moment in front of her. 'You coming along boss? I'll fill you in on what we know on the way, which is precious little.'

Glad of the action to keep her mind occupied Lorraine nodded. 'Right,' she turned to the car the constables were in. 'Give me one minute to sign in,' the driver nodded.

Back outside, she threw her keys at Carter. 'We'll take my car. Come on Carter, you drive. I need to catch up with Luke and make a few phone calls in the way.'

Obligingly Carter caught the keys and hurried to Lorraine's car, quickly he jumped into the driver's seat.

They set off following the squad car as it sped towards Sunderland with flashing lights and screaming sirens. In the back Lorraine looked at Luke and smiled. 'Right what's it all about?'

'Young man, found dead on the roof of the glass centre, basically that's all we know, and Scottie's on his way, actually seeing as he's closer he'll probably be there before we are.'

'No identification yet?'

'No-nothing other than what I've just told you.'

Lorraine nodded and turned her head to look out of the window.

Watching her Luke felt his heart skip, outwardly the week on Holy Island had done her some good, but she'd been distant since the incident of her kidnapping had happened. And this morning, well she'd certainly left him with a lump in his throat.

He sighed, hoping that her getting back to work would take her mind of everything. She had opened up a little bit while they had been away, probably due to the peace and tranquillity of Holy Island, he shuddered, if he could only get his hands round the bastard's throat. That twat would be the one getting the peace and tranquillity. At least, thanks to Loraine's courage, the lousy bastard was now behind bars and unable to hurt and disfigure any other women.

Luke had been protective all of his life, especially of anything smaller than himself, which was probably half the human race and most animals, he couldn't help it, it's the way he was.

When they pulled up in the car park beside the glass roof of the centre, it was to find that a small crowd had gathered, and Scottie's team dressed in white coveralls were already at work. Scottie was a big man, just a shade taller than Luke, but more on the heavy side, with a mane of jet back hair. Body hair peeked out of the top of his collar and the sleeves of his coverall. He waved at them from the roof, which was reachable by a small incline leading up from the car park. In the middle the incline parted and led downwards to the entrance of the centre.

Taking a white suit and blue shoe covers from Scottie's aide a young man named Sam, of obvious Chinese decent who everyone liked, and who wore a pair of rimless glasses. Lorraine quickly put the suit and shoe covers on; a moment later she stepped onto the roof with a slight smile, knowing that behind her Luke would be wondering where to put his feet.

'Hello my love,' pleased to see Loraine as usual and smiling Scottie patted her arm. 'Looking good as always pet. And I'm really pleased you're back where you belong. Oh by the way, Edna was asking after you the other day.'

'Thanks Scottie, reckon I'll see her soon. Oh and thanks for the compliment.'

'Of course, my dear, don't you always look good enough to eat.' Scottie grinned and glanced back at Luke. For a moment his jaw dropped, as he stared at him.

'You catching fly's Scottie?' Lorraine smiled.

Scottie shook his head, and with a grin went on. 'Oh my God I don't bloody well believe it...What the hell's he doing?'

Lorraine spun round, and the smile became a laugh, Luke was imitating with his foot the way Duke had been waving his paw over the water less than an hour ago.

'Didn't know you were frightened of heights mate?' Scottie said, and unable to stop himself, laughed loudly.

'He is a bit Scottie, well a big bit. You should see him on a plane, that's bad, enough...But here, he just can't seem to get his head around walking on glass twenty feet up in the air.'

Luke pulled a face at them both as he very cautiously put his right foot on the roof, then making sure that each foot was placed carefully on the edge of each pane, and keeping his eyes right in front of him and using a swaggering cowboy gait, he finally reached Lorraine and Scottie.

'It's not natural man!' He glared at Scottie.

'Never.' Scottie said, trying hard not to laugh.

Lorraine was looking the other way.

'Like I've said before if we were meant to be up in the air, we would have friggin' wings.'

Shaking her head and trying to keep the amusement out of her face, Lorraine turned back to Scottie. 'Found out anything so far then, Scottie?'

'Well, actually I just got here a few minutes or so before you lot did. Accident slowed us down,' he glanced at the body and grimaced. 'But I know enough to say it's definitely murder, no chance of it being suicide the poor bugger's been scalped, and he's literally bled to death.'

'Scalped...' Lorraine stepped back in shock. 'Well that's a first for me. Jesus Christ,' she stared at the dead man's back and slowly shook her head. 'Poor sod.'

'Scalped.' Carter echoed, showing none of Luke's aversion to walking on the glass roof as he stared down in awe at the blood soaked corpse.

A moment later, followed closely by Carter, Lorraine walked around the body, stopping and staring from each angle. Behind her Carter kept swallowing, praying that he would not be sick, not sharing Luke's fear of heights he did however have a slight aversion to large amounts of blood.

'Right then, looks like there's not a lot we can do here at the moment,' Lorraine looked up at Scottie after a few minutes, before glancing at her watch. 'I'll pay you a visit in a couple of hours, maybe's three, by the time we get back and sort a few things out...Like is this a one off, or is there more, or are there going to be anymore.' She shrugged. 'Is that alright with you Scottie?'

Scottie glanced at his own watch. 'Well, I have an eighty year old man who thought he could beat a lorry and reach the other side of the road before it was on top of him, turns out he was wrong, and a fifteen year old girl on the slab with not one but two needles in her arm. Both pretty straight forward. So yeah, we should know a bit more about this case by then.'

'Alright, we'll be off.' Lorraine smiled at Scottie.

'Cheers love...Oh, and mind how you go Luke; it's a long way to the bottom.' He grinned at Luke.

'Aye right.' Luke scowled at him, as he carefully placed one foot in front of the other and with a sigh of relief when he reached the edge quickly stepped off the roof.

Lorraine put the five PC's two of Sunderland's and the three of her own, on search and guard, before heading with Luke and Carter towards the car.

## CHAPTER FIFTEEN

'I'm sorry.' He mumbled. 'Really I'm sorry...Please God if you're really there. If you do exist...I'm sorry.

A tear slid down his face, even though he'd thought himself all cried out.

He was apologising to God for the time he'd been to blame for the death of their pet dog, and had blamed his brother even though he'd only been six years old when it happened. He had not known how deep Joe's pond was when he'd thrown the stick for Spot, their jack Russell to fetch, even though their father had shouted 'No.' At the time.

That was just one of the many things he'd apologised for over the last few hours,

And that was it, he thought. Hours.

How many did he have left?

He sniffed the air.

Still breathable, no rotten smell apart from the damp, but what did that mean?

If anything I might have a few more hours?

Or less?

So much I haven't done.

So much yet to see.

'I'm sorry.' He said yet again. It had turned into a prayer which as the minutes ticked away he would keep on repeating, over and over.

## CHAPTER SIXTEEN

Twenty minutes later they were back in the station; Lorraine pulled the tab on a can of diet coke, as she sat on the corner of her desk and filled Sanderson and Dinwall in on what they had seen at the Glass centre.

Sanderson, an old family friend of Lorraine's mother, and who had always been like an uncle to Lorraine, his hair thinning and greying at an alarming rate, and who had watched Lorraine's climb up the ladder in the police force with pride, leaned his back against his desk with his arms folded across his chest the fingers of his right hand tapping against his left elbow.

'Hmm.' Dinwall turned to his computer. His long dark hair hung in a pony tail tied at the back of his neck, he wore a white cotton shirt with a black leather waistcoat. 'Nothing,' he said raising his hands palm up, 'no mention anywhere of a friggin mad scalper running wild.'

'So you reckon it's his first victim?' Lorraine asked. 'It's certainly the first I've heard of.'

Sanderson shrugged. 'For all we know there could be bodies

scattered all over Northumberland and Durham. Even bloody Yorkshire.'

'And,' Luke quickly put in. 'He's so good at hiding them this is the very first one to be found.'

'So you think this guy might be the one, after God knows how many that finally got away. And nearly made it to safety?' Lorraine raised her eyebrows.

'Could be...But why? Why would anyone go to such lengths, and for what reason?' Luke asked.'

'To frighten others off,' Sanderson said. 'I mean can you think of a better way?'

Luke shook his head. 'Not really.'

'Hmm...' Lorraine nodded. 'Worth thinking about Sanderson, but we'll see what Scottie has to say later.'

'Anything found on or around the body?' Sanderson asked. Lifting his head and looking at Lorraine.

She shook her head. 'Not that we know of, and certainly not while we were there Sanderson...So, seeing as there's very little we can do about it until we do get a chance to talk to Scottie...It's time someone filled me in on these new people staying in the safe house.'

Stepping away from the desk, Sanderson said. 'Before that Boss, I've just remembered, there was an incident a canny few years ago of a scalper in Hetton Le Hole, scalped a whole family, all three of them, the father and two or three brothers,' Sanderson tapped his fingers on top of a pile of files. 'Or was it just the three brothers?'

'What?' Luke said. 'How come I've never heard about it?'

'How long ago?' Lorraine asked. 'I mean something like that you'd think everyone would know about. Was it kept hush, hush or what?'

'Don't think so, and it's gotta be forty years or more. Over time, people tend to forget.'

'What?' Dinwall echoed Luke.

'But he'll be.' Luke frowned.

'Old?' Sanderson put in, with a raised eyebrow.

Lorraine nodded.

'Well, depends what you mean by old. Apparently he was only sixteen at the time, big lad...Very big, so they say, they reckon he drugged the lot of them- then did the job... Actually he might be out of prison by now.'

'So he's fifty six then, might be still strong enough. That's if he's looked after himself.' Luke said.

'But why? Got a name for him?' Lorraine looked at Sanderson.

'It's on the tip of me flaming tongue, just can't remember it...

It was a long time ago, something to do with his sisters I think.'

Lorraine turned to Dinwall. 'Run a check.'

'It's running Boss.'

They all moved over to Dinwall and his computer. 'That's him.' Lorraine pointed at the screen and frowned as two photographs, one of Grossmont as a young man, and one of him on his release, stared back at her.

'Alfred Harold Grossmont released two months ago today.' Luke read from the screen. 'Forty one years for three murders. Hmm, he must have had a damn good brief to get out of there at all. Or...Some bloody idiot do-gooder thinks he's been in the clink long enough. Can you believe it?'

'Should have thrown the key away,' Sanderson said quietly. 'And from what I vaguely remember, the lad was very lucky to make it into police custody.'

Lorraine gave him a puzzled glance.

'Probably have taken his age and other factors into consideration, like why it all happened in the first place,' Dinwall frowned. 'He must have had a reason, well...In his friggin crazy mind like.'

'Would have to be one hell of a bloody reason for God's sake.' Sanderson glared at him.

Lorraine looked at Sanderson. Wondering what the hell was

up with these two, it's like I'm in a parallel universe where these two have switched roles. She looked at them both again. Usually it was the mild mannered Sanderson who was willing to give people the benefit of the doubt, lately though he seemed quite irritable...And of course Dinwall will always say the opposite to Sanderson, whatever the issue.

'That's his name...Defiantly him.' Sanderson snapped his fingers. 'It's coming back now, from what I remember the motive *was* revenge and a spur of the moment thing. The lad was known in the town as a gentle giant, his head always in books, and a smile on his face. Apparently his teachers had high hopes for him. Anyhow they, the ones he murdered, lived next door and one night three of the sons, it definitely was the sons, raped his poor mother and two of his younger sisters repeatedly, the sisters were only twelve and nine at the time.'

'Bastards!' Lorraine said.

'Yes,' Sanderson agreed, before going on. 'The lad sort of lost it. Made some kind of drug concoction and used his mother's insulin needles to inject them. Took him a couple of days, but he got them, one by one and stacked them up in his mother's washhouse. They were found when a few days later a house to house was organised. It wouldn't have been many more days before the neighbours would have been complaining about the smell anyhow, can you imagine if it had been around summer time...Three of them.'

'Oh.' Dinwall grimaced. 'I can actually smell it now.'

'Doubt that.' Sanderson said.

'Didn't he make any attempt to hide the body's...Other than in the washhouse?' Luke asked.

'Well,' Sanderson went on, 'I suppose he was at the time a very naive sixteen year old. God only knew what was going on in his head. Like I said, I wasn't part of the investigation, so really all I can remember is the gossip at the time. And the fact that most of Hetton wanted him to get off with it.'

'What about the mother and the sisters?' Luke pulled a chair up, crossed his legs and rubbed his right knee. 'Are they all still living in the area?'

Sanderson shrugged. 'I can't really remember much off hand. It was my first year as a cop, just a wee nobody on the beat. And actually the lad did have quite a lot of sympathy in the village, from what I remember the rapists were a right rotten bunch. A lot of people who they had bullied one way or another, were pleased to see the back of them trust me, evil bunch...Should have shot the whole lousy family.'

Again Lorraine gave him a puzzled glance; Sanderson had not been acting Sanderson like, since the year had turned. And recently after a ten year break he'd started smoking again. She'd puzzled this over with Luke, but neither of them could figure out why, or even what could possibly be wrong with the usually mild mannered detective. She was reluctant to ask him, but she was starting to worry about him, perhaps a word with her mother, maybes she might know what's going on with him. They had been best friends for a long time.

She walked slowly back to her desk, and took a sip of diet coke, before asking. 'So, where's Grossmont been living since he got out?'

Dinwall scrolled down the screen, then looked over to Lorraine. 'He's living in sheltered accommodation in Morpeth boss, obviously part of his release conditions are that he's not allowed anywhere near Hetton Le Hole. Some of the victims family, cousins and such, still live there. His own immediate family, mother and the two sisters involved moved, first down to Cornwell where there are other relatives, then back up here to Corbridge... ten years ago, last month.'

'What about the father?'

'He died a year after the incident. Apparently he drank himself to death.'

'Right, Sanderson, you and Dinwall, pay Morpeth police a visit, liaison with them and bring this Alfred Grossmont in. We need to talk to him. You sure he's the only one in the area, who's ever been accused of scalping?'

Dinwall shrugged. 'I'll do a wider search when we get back. But can't see there being anymore, Jesus, the thoughts of one, merry scalper on the loose is enough.'

Sanderson frowned at him, really, he thought; Dinwall certainly needs a few lessons in etiquette. Uncouth doesn't cut it. His frown deepened.

Seeing the frown, Lorraine turned back to Dinwall. 'Right then, you do that, when you get back not now.' She quickly added as Dinwall turned back to his computer.

For a moment Dinwall hesitated not looking forward to the forty minute journey cooped up with Sanderson, who was thinking pretty much the same about Dinwall.

'So what are youse two waiting for...A hug?'

'Okay boss.' Both men echoed as they quickly slipped their jackets on.

When they had gone, Lorraine said to Luke. 'I thought you were going to get that knee seen too?'

Luke shook his head. 'It's getting better. No point in bothering the doctors, is there?'

'You should have at least let me strap it up.'

'It's fine.'

Lorraine grinned. As well as a distinct fear of heights, Luke also had a deep distrust of doctors. 'I suppose that'll teach you not to show off and pretend you can do the bloody twist. But you did give everyone in the pub that night, a damn good laugh when you eventually hit the ground.' She laughed out loud at the picture in her head.

'Well, you know how it is, one too many, and all that,' he winked at her. 'Sure to do it every time.'

'Right then,' Lorraine moved to the office window. 'Fill me in on what Carter has to say about the new tenants on the Seahills. Not the full version, like what colour clothes they all were wearing, and what they had on their feet, cos I'm sure he'll have noted it, just what I need to hear.'

Before he could tell her, Lorraine's office phone rang. She went back to her desk. After a moment she said. 'Yes.' She waved her arm around desperately trying not to punch the air. Putting the phone down, she grinned at Luke. 'They've only gone and caught that bastard. Billy Hardy.'

'Finally,' Luke did punch the air. 'Yes.'

'Come on.' Lorraine stood up. 'Clark wants us to do the interrogating.'

Hardy had been under Lorraine's skin for a while, three times she'd had him in custody, each time he'd wriggled free, once on a technicality the others with the aid of sworn witnesses.

She vowed to herself as she closed the door. There will not be a fourth time.

Hardy was one vile creature and this time he was going to pay, couldn't give a shit who the bastard is friends with.

## CHAPTER SEVENTEEN

Sarah Rose Sinclaire was more than terrified; she sat facing the man with the scar on his face. It seemed ages since he'd sat down in front of her, it seemed forever since she had ran her fingers through the sand.

The one who had brought her here with his big cuddly dog-the one who had promised and fed her Pizza, the one who she had willingly came with, was gone now. He had stroked the side of her face, and kissed it as he felt her breast. She had lashed out with her foot, but laughing he had jumped out of the way.

When she had screamed, 'Fuck off,' at him. He had laughed even louder.

Blowing her a kiss at the door, he had said. 'See you soon.'

That had been ages ago, might be hours, she had no way of knowing, her watch, her phone, her purse; everything had been taken from her.

He stared at her a twisted sneer on his face, which enhanced the scar, making him look truly evil. Finally he said. 'You'll do.'

'Fuck you...Let me go.'

'No can do.'

Suddenly he rose out of his chair and slapped her across her face.

She screamed. 'I hate you, let me go.'

'Hate a lot of people do you?'

'Fuck off.'

'Only I've come to realise in my line of work, just how spoilt brats like you react.'

Leaning over he stroked her hand, quickly she pulled it away, her eyes full of tears, her heart full of fear.

## CHAPTER EIGHTEEN

They walked down the corridor to a room that was three doors away from theirs. Entering they sat down facing Hardy, shaven headed and muscle bound, he sneered at both of them in turn, before spitting in the direction of Lorraine's feet.

Lorraine kicked his shin under the table. 'Alright you pathetic scumbag, talk.'

'Fuck off.' Although the kick must have hurt, Hardy didn't even blink.

'Nice.'

'I want a solicitor.'

'Oh so you need one do you?'

He glared at her, from under dark eyelashes which any woman would die for. His eyes dark and predatory bored into her. Hardy was a very handsome man. He used his charm to cheat any woman-young or old, out of their possessions, if his charm didn't work then he used his fists, and took what he wanted. Often leaving them alone and bleeding.

'No comment.'

Staring at Hardy, Luke put his elbows on the table, crossed his fingers and rested his chin on them

Ignoring Hardy, Lorraine read from the file in front of her, then passed it over to Luke.

'So creep, it looks like you picked the wrong woman this time scumbag. Janette Monrose has made a full statement, saying you took her home from the Blue Lion last night, after you had sex and when she didn't fall for your sob story. What was it this time, oh yes. Your mother is dying and you needed a couple of hundred to get to London to see her on her death bed...And, when Mrs Monroe refused, you beat her up and stole fifty quid from her purse. Nice one. Scumbag.'

'Wasn't me.'

Luke looked up at the ceiling, muttering. 'Course it wasn't.'

Lorraine laughed, just before she kicked him again. 'Lying evil twat. You deliberately prey on women who won't come forward, because they fear being labelled as a prostitute or at the very least an easy woman.'

'I want a solicitor.'

Lorraine leaned forward. 'Pity...We don't always get what we want arsehole.'

'I know my rights lovely.' He reached over and attempted to stroke Lorraine's hand.

'Go on I dare you.'

Slowly his eyes locked with hers, he withdrew his hand.

Lorraine's eyes bored into him as he smirked at her, Luke stood up and went to the side of the table, putting himself between them. Leaning over the table until his face was an inch away from Hardy's, he looked him in the eye. 'Try that again,' he threatened. 'And-your solicitor is on her way.'

Hardy sat back in his chair and folded his arms across his chest. His eyes flicked towards Luke. Looked him up and down, before saying sarcastically. 'Youse two coppers an item, or what?' he grinned at them both.

Lorraine banged her fist on the table, as Hardy quickly moved his legs out of her reach. 'We ask the questions in here,' she leaned forward, staring into his eyes. 'Fucking moron.'

'Yeah,' he shrugged.

'Yeah,' Luke echoed. 'And don't forget it.'

There was a knock on the door and the duty solicitor, Megan Cawly entered the room.

Lorraine gestured for Luke to start the tape. When the formalities were over, she again asked Hardy what he knew of Janette Monroe.

'No comment.'

Lorraine took the folder off Luke, glanced inside for a

moment, before saying. 'And I'm guessing there's no comment to be made about the dog fighting you arrange out of the Blue Lion either?'

For a moment his face went pale. 'No comment.'

Hmm, Lorraine thought, guess he's more frightened of dobbing Mrs Archer in, than any of the woman he's hurt.

'Let's face it; you're nothing but a fucking scumbag, aren't you? Pompous nasty git.'

Luke gently touched the side of Lorraine's leg, but she was in no mood to go easy. Her first day back was proving to be one hell of a day and it wasn't even noon yet.

'So, you send kids out to nick pet dogs, badly treat them and use them for dog fighting?'

'No need to answer,' his solicitor said. 'That's a totally different offence, without proof.'

Hardy again stared arrogantly at Lorraine. 'No comment.'

'So you deny all charges.'

'Yes.'

'Do you deny this evidence?' Lorraine slipped photographs out of the folder and spread them in front of him. The photographs were of Hardy assaulting Janette Monroe. 'Still denying it?'

'But...But this is a set up...Got to be, never seen the woman before...Honestly.'

'Oh please, is that the best you've got.'

'It wasn't me.'

'Her daughter, Mr Hardy, her fourteen year old daughter took the pictures, she heard everything, and slipped outside and took the photos through the window.'

For a moment he was quiet as he stared at Lorraine, his intention to intimidate failed as staring right back at him, she said. 'What we like to call banged to rights Mr Hardy. Guess your career is well and truly over. You Mr Hardy are under arrest for grievous bodily harm, on more than one account. Read him his rights DS Daniels.'

She stood and went to the door. Turning she said. 'Oh, and the dog fighting,' she smiled. 'That's ongoing. Plenty of puppy lovers where you're going, one word, that's all it will take you can guess the result.'

Outside she leaned against the wall and took a deep breath. A feeling of deep satisfaction coursed through her veins.

'Another evil bastard down,' she muttered as she made her way to her office.

## CHAPTER NINETEEN

The woman silently stared out of the window as she washed the dishes, dreaming of a different life that was so far out of reach it might as well have been on another planet, a life that was never ever coming back- a life that belonged to another woman, another time, another place.

A life that she thought of constantly, a life that was in every silent tear she cried. Gently she raised her hand and touched her face, for a moment her hand was still then her fingers ran over her bruised cheek. There were more bruises, running around her neck, an unmoving necklace coloured in the jewel colours of red, purple and blue.

'You're late,' a man's voice shouted, startling her, she froze her body pressing against the sink as he moved closer. She felt his breath on her neck as he said. 'How many times do you have to be told? You English, so fucking the idiots, you too good for woman's work? Eh-eh?' He prodded her stiff back, with an even stiffer middle finger

'No no.' she said quickly.

Tall, thickset, dark haired with a deep knife scar, running from the corner of his right eye down to his mouth, which raised his lip in a permanent sneer, and wearing a pair of large dark framed glasses. He walked back to the door, turned and glared at her just before he slammed it. Two other men, already seated at the table, talking amongst themselves barley gave her a glance, as he moved back and stood behind her, again trapping her against the sink. Spinning her around to face him he squeezed her right breast hard.

Her body flinched as she muttered. 'Sorry,'

Quickly drying her hands she slipped out of his reach and ran over to the big cupboard on the other side of the large gloomy kitchen. She took out six cereal bowls, grabbed a box of cornflakes, hurried back to the table and spread the bowls out.

All the time he was watching her.

Placing the cornflakes in the middle, she went back to the large bench, took spoons out of the drawer and picked a bowl of sugar up. Still he silently watched her.

Inside she was trembling, it was not unusual for him to swipe the bowls and cereal off the table, throw her on top of it and use her in front of the other men.

One after another, five more men each one of them looking her up and down and undressing her with their eyes, and the one she hated and feared the most, even more than Scarface, the one who the others called Draco blew kisses at her when they came into the kitchen and took their places at the table as she dropped slices of bread into the toaster.

She carried on with her work, her face showing no interest as they discussed their plans for today.

Her mind though, was as keen and sharp as it had ever been.

She remembered everything that had been said in the kitchen over the last three months, every detail and every name.

Would she ever be able to use it?

Would she ever find the courage to escape this hell hole where others much braver than her, had tried and failed?

## CHAPTER TWENTY

Melanie Musgrove spotted Dev coming out of the shop; with a sharp gasp she threw herself behind the wall of the end house in Daffodil crescent, praying with trembling lips that he had not seen her. After a minute she crept to the edge of the wall, and crossing her fingers, she peeped out terrified in case he was still there, and wondering what she would do if he was. With another gasp she quickly jumped back. He was just about to walk past her.

Dev, dark haired, and lean, could be called handsome if he did not look permanently angry, had arrived on the Seahills estate fresh from prison, four months ago, only one person knew who he was and where he had come from, no one had seen that person for a long while now.

Slowly, starting to feel sick, and with her heart beat rising by the moment she looked around the edge of the wall again, and breathed easily a moment later when there was no sign of him. Dev had frightened her before by holding a knife to her throat, but after her dad Jacko collared him, he also went missing. The nightmares had only just stopped.

No one knew where he had disappeared too, she remembered Sandra saying that he was probably licking his wounds somewhere like the dog he was, and her nana had said the same.

She hadn't quite understood what they had meant and had pictures in her mind of him licking his face and arms; it was her friend Emma who had said it was just a saying.

But now he was back!

She stepped away from the wall and still frightened in case he suddenly popped up, she swung her head from left to right, taking in the empty street.

'He, he might be hiding somewhere,' she muttered, as she slowly, practically forcing each leg in front of her walked to the shop, wondering if she should run or not, or even go home without her grandmother's bag of sugar.

'She'll go off it if I don't get the sugar.'

'Better get the sugar.' She nodded to herself.

Stepping inside, it suddenly occurred to her that he might have gone back into the shop. She froze, and quietly, tears of fear forming in her eyes, said the shopkeepers name. 'Mr Jansen...Mr Jansen.'

What if he's hiding? This thought frightened her even more, as she quickly looked around.

Again she shouted the shop keeper's name. There was no

answer as Melanie held her breath and strained to listen for the slightest sound. Slowly she put one foot after the other and tip toed down the central isle.

'Mr Jansen,' she said, louder this time, as she approached the counter, 'Mr Jansen,' her hands trembling as she reached for the counter to steady herself, she looked over the top, then gasped. Mr Jansen was lying very still on the floor, his face covered in blood.

Screaming Melanie ran out of the shop.

## CHAPTER TWENTY ONE

The new people staying at the safe house, Fiona and her children were heading towards the corner shop when Molly spotted the swing park. With a squeal of excitement she broke into a run only to be grabbed by her mother.

'Molly! I've told you never ever run off from me. How many times, will you please do as you're told?'

'But mum, I'm only gonna have a go on the swings. Please mum...Pretty please.'

'Yes well, we'll go together. And it's going not gonna. Really how many times do I have to tell you?'

Molly pulled a face behind her mother's back.

'Is it alright now?' She demanded, when they were within a yard of the swings.

'Don't be clever, madam.'

'Mum.' Oliver said.

'What?' she snapped at him.

Saying nothing Oliver just stared at her for a moment then moved his eyes to his sister.

Shaking her head Fiona apologised. 'Sorry Molly...I've got a lot on my mind,' she patted Molly's arm. 'I'll get some chocolate and we'll watch a film eh?'

Molly flung her arms around Fiona. 'It's alright mum...I shouldn't be cheeky... Can I pick the film?'

'Course you can.'

'Mum.'

'What Molly?'

'When's dad coming home?' She stepped back and looked up at her mother. 'You said he would meet us at the new house, so where is he?'

Fiona, totally distracted, pulled her phone out for the fiftieth time that morning, still no message from her husband or her brother, so much for I'll ring in a couple of hours. Putting it back in her pocket she said. 'What...Oh yes, soon Molly, soon...Go on have ten minutes on the swings.'

As Molly jumped on the first swing, Oliver followed Fiona onto the seat. She looked at him her eyes questioning, guessing what was coming and wondering how long she could keep the truth from him, she said flatly. 'What?'

'Okay mum I'm not stupid this is the second house we've been in, in a week. On a lousy council estate, a place you said you would never step foot on in your whole life, remember...

Something's going on.'

Fiona patted Oliver's arm, much in the way she had patted Molly's. 'It's nothing for you to worry about son.'

'I think it is mum,' he hesitated a moment shuffling his feet in the grass. 'It's about what happened that night isn't it...I know, I've seen things like this on the telly...We're on the run.'

Fiona's heart skipped a beat, no way should her children be put through all of this, and have their whole lives turned upside down. She should have known that Oliver would put it all together, he was far from stupid.

What to say to him?

How to explain it all?

She clenched her hands around the wooden bench. If the worst happened she was ready to just up and go. A new life, a new country, not what she really wanted. She loved her husband and her brother in law, but her children came first and if she had to, she would sacrifice the first two for the latter two. Money was no problem she could get her hands on plenty.

'Who's running?' Molly had sneaked up without either of them seeing her.

Startled, Fiona quickly said as she threw Oliver a stern glance. 'No one's running love, your brother was just kidding on. He says he can run faster than me.'

'I can run faster than you mum,' Molly laughed, 'so can the all the snails.'

'Yes very funny; come on then let's get some shopping in for lunch, then this afternoon, we'll use my lap top to check out your new schools. Now that should be exiting.'

Both of them groaned. 'Do we really have to?' Oliver looked defiantly at his mother.

'Oh yes. Come on.' She gave his shoulder a warning squeeze.

'Can we have spaghetti?' Molly asked.

'You can have anything you want darling.' Fiona answered. She was too busy looking furtively around her to notice the strange look her son gave her.

Then all three stopped and stared with puzzled frowns as a young girl screaming for her dad ran past them.

## CHAPTER TWENTY TWO

Dev sat down on a patch of grass, his back against the brick wall of the end house facing the swing park. He took the lid off the milk and swigged the lot, throwing the empty bottle onto the grass, wondering how long it would be before word spread around here that he was back.

His face twisted into a sneer as he muttered. 'And this time I ain't taking no prisoners,' rolling a cigarette he paused a moment when he heard a door slam and a deep male voice shouting 'Fuck off cow.'

A second later a female voice, yelled. 'No you fuck off you cheating lousy scumbag. And that's what you really are, no fucking good to anyone, you never have been, never will be, even your own mother said the same. And you're a fucking greedy twat as well... go on piss of back to that ugly tart you've been shagging behind my back, you fucking pervy creep.'

'Don't worry. I fucking well will.'

'Will you now?'

'Oh yes.'

'You fucking dare go to hers.'

Make your fucking mind up. Dev thought. Grinning to himself, as the couple came into sight. Dev did a double take, as they continued to throw insults at each other. They were the most ill matched couple he had ever seen. The man a small, dark and squat, Asian, in black jeans and grey sweatshirt with a navy holdall slung over his shoulder, was towered over by the very tall stick thin blonde still in her yellow pyjamas and red dressing gown.

Dev made himself comfortable for the floor show.

'You gonna stop me like? Cos believe me she's a better lay than you any day, beats me why I stayed so fucking long here anyhow. To be honest you're fucking useless. And those kids will be better off without a mother like you, selfish cow.'

'I'm warning you, I'll fucking kill the both of you. I mean it. You dare leave me for her.'

The man laughed. 'Fuck off lazy cow.'

'Me lazy?'

'Yes you.'

'Says the bastard who's never worked a day in his fucking life.'

'Get stuffed. Enough's enough. Fed up and can't take no fucking more of your constant winging all bloody day. Your fucking neighbours should know just how two faced and nasty you really are. Bitch.' He turned to walk away.

For a moment there was silence then the woman screamed. 'Don't go Arun, please don't go.'

'Make your fucking mind up.'

'Please Arun.' The woman cried. 'Please don't leave me you know I love you.'

Turning back he stared at her for a moment before shaking his head. 'No I've had enough to last a life time, fuck off you pathetic druggie. Even I wouldn't stoop as low as you do to get a fix....You dirty filthy bitch.'

'Please, please, don't leave me...Not for her. Please,' she begged over and over.

'Fuck off.' He jerked his arm from her grip.

The woman screamed again as Arun turned his back on her, she grabbed at his holdall in a vain attempt to keep him there, but with a hefty shove he pushed her away and ignoring her cry's, continued on down the street with a determined stride, passing Dev without even seeing him.

Dev watched as the woman, bare footed, with blood oozing between the toes of her right foot ran after him, all the time screaming for him to wait up, but her heart rendering pleas were falling on deaf ears. When she reached Arun he turned and punched her in her mouth. 'Shut up and fuck off.'

The woman fell to her knees in the gutter sobbing her heart out, begging for Arun to come back.

Dev pulled his knees up and buried his head between his legs, replaying a similar scene in his head. The pictures that he had long suppressed crowded his mind so much that his head hurt.

'Why?' He muttered as he wiped his eyes.

'Why me?'

He used a match to light his cigarette took a deep draw, and ran the match over the back of his hand. Greedily the flame licked at his skin. Dev held his breath until the flame died. The tears came again as he held his hand to his chest.

'Why me?' He muttered again.

'Why me?'

## CHAPTER TWENTY THREE

She had began clearing the table as the men left the kitchen, because after she was finished in here she had been ordered to clean one of the bedrooms and to make sure that every trace of blood was eliminated as quickly as possible or she would be sorry, the word sorry implemented with a hard vicious squeeze of her right breast again the one he favoured time and time again, by the one she hated the most. She shuddered as his back disappeared through the door, wondering yet again just what was waiting for her in the bedroom.

She sucked in her breath and held it, refusing to give into despair. She breathed deeply again.

'One day.' She muttered.

It was the only thing that kept her going, the thought that one day she would get out of here. And now once more with the dishes, and her hands in the water, she stared out of the kitchen window at nothing. Three yards from the window was a high brick wall which went up the length of the house, she had counted each brick numerous times, watched bird-shit appear on certain bricks and watched it wash away again with the rain. Only to be repeated the next day, or the next...Or the next.

Once, she had forgotten when, although now she only measured time by the sun and the stars, but it felt like forever, because each day in here *was* forever, she had seen a man she didn't know in the yard. Without thinking it through, and out of sheer desperation, she had climbed onto the sink and managing to get the old sash window open, she had got the top half of her body out and yelled over and over for help.

That had been a terrible mistake, the man had laughed loudly at her and shouted to those inside the house, a minute later she was grabbed from behind and pulled back inside, her head banged off the corner of the window hard enough to stun her, then three of them had raped and beaten her until she could hardly stand up, when they had finally left her, a picture of them walking away rubbing their hands and laughing was never far from her mind, she had crawled into a corner to die. And she had, not physically, but die she had.

Sometime that day or the next a strange woman who never spoke and never listened to anyone, even on the coldest nights she kept to her own space and never used the others for warmth, had came in and bathed the crusted blood from her body, then helped her onto a large dog bed in the walk in cupboard and threw a filthy smelly blanket over her. She came everyday for the next week and kindly fed her soup.

This memory was interrupted when the boss man came in and slapped a blood soaked carrier bag on the table. 'Clean that up and hang it with the rest.'

When he had gone she stared at the bag, knowing what was inside, but silently praying and begging it did not belong to someone she knew, a certain someone who in the dead of night had whispered to her that he was going to escape. And that he would come back for her.

## CHAPTER TWENTY FOUR

'Hello Edna'. Lorraine said as she walked into Scottie's domain with Luke and Carter close behind her. She swallowed hard as the metallic chemical smell of the morgue hit her as it always did.

'Well hello yourself'. Edna replied with a grin, pushing her glasses back up her nose, as she turned back to her sticky labels and test tubes. Edna had jumped up the ladder from being Scottie's landlady to his surrogate mother years ago, she had also worked with him for a long time, they lived together in Durham and well past retiring age, she still came into work most mornings. Secretly Scottie dreaded the day it all became too much for her, knowing that she really was irreplaceable.

Lorraine and Luke walked over to the autopsy table, while Carter not really knowing where to go hovered by the door. Lorraine stared sadly down for a moment at the dead man. She sighed thinking, who are you?

Where do you come from?

Are your family looking for you?

Praying for you?

A few hours ago his features had been hard to see; now she was looking at a young man who had yesterday been quite handsome. But that young man was no more. She looked at Scottie, the question in her eyes.

'Well...As you can see my dear he's in his early twenties. Cause of death, scalping. The shame of it is my dear, a few weeks ago, that's before the weather turned for the better- he probably, well; could have survived...'

'What?' Luke said quickly. 'You can survive being scalped?'

'It's been known to happen.'

'How the hell can you survive that?' Lorraine asked, holding her hands palm upwards, in amazement.

At the door Carter gulped and tried hard not to be sick, the thought of someone being scalped turned his stomach, especially since he was relatively new to the autopsy room. And this, he felt queasy, this was not something he'd not been prepared for. Hell, anything but this!

Scottie went on. 'How it works is, if the weather was really cold like near freezing, it would help slow the flow of blood. And, if the cut was jagged as this one is and not just sliced but half torn off,' Lorraine winced as Scottie went on. 'Then the arteries constrict faster slowing the flow of blood, so with quick medical help.' He shrugged, indicating that it would still be touch and go, but a chance of survival was there.

'Well...That's very interesting Scottie. But we are talking about a very strong man, to do this...'

'Or more than one, do you think?' Luke frowned.

'Either a very strong man, or a couple of mere mortals, either is possible.' Scottie looked from Luke to Lorraine.

Lorraine tapped her fingers on the edge of the steel trolley, not wanting to go down the route of more than one perp for the moment. 'So got anything else for us? Like what the hell he was doing on the roof of the glass centre, and just who the hell he is?' Lorraine looked up at Scottie.

'What he was doing on the roof my dear, not a clue, who he is, or where he's from originally. I can't tell you that either, well not yet, although I can however tell you that I'm nearly certain he's not British.'

'Migrant worker, do you think...Perhaps?' Luke said, looking up from the body to Scottie.

Scottie shrugged. 'There was no identification of any sort on him, all that was in his pockets was a packet of Russian cigarettes and a cheap plastic lighter. I'm waiting for DNA tests to come through- but I'm pretty sure he's Rumanian.'

'Illegal, perhaps?' Lorraine was still frowning at the body, but glanced quickly at Scottie.

Looking at Lorraine, Scottie nodded his head. 'Also he has quite a few old scars on him.' Turning back to the body Scottie rolled the white sheet down. He pointed to a jagged scar on the left hand side of his chest. 'See here, it looks like he's had a few broken ribs, and at least one has penetrated the skin. That would have taken an exceptional blow. And here another scar on his thigh looks like an old knife wound to me. There's a matching one on his right arm. Also his back is covered with what looks like a series of recent whip lashes.'

'Whip lashes.' Carter gagged by the door.

'Punishment?' Lorraine frowned.

'Well...Or he could be a masochist.' Scottie moved his head from side to side.

'But you don't think so.'

'Could have been?' Carter muttered from the doorway.

They all turned round and looked at him. 'I mean...He could be, couldn't he...I mean...'

'Yes we know what you mean Carter,' Lorraine turned back to Scottie. 'Carry on.'

'Given the other wounds, not really,' he shook his head. 'A few of the scars are quite old, possibly, well they most probably happened in childhood, though a few are quite recent, months, weeks, previous to the scalping.'

'And you reckon he's only in his early twenties?'

'Yes.'

'Poor sod.' Luke muttered.

'Okay, then really we have nothing to go on do we?'

'Not a lot.'

'Time of death?'

'I would say early hours of this morning- sometime between three and six.'

Unable to stop himself, Carter muttered. 'Poor sod.'

'So how come no one noticed him before?' Lorraine shook her head. 'How come I didn't notice him, fucking hell I drove past the flaming place...I mean he's actually lying spread-eagled on a roof, for God's sake.' She slapped her forehead and looked at Luke, 'Can't bloody well believe it.'

'Not your ordinary roof though is it... And it's amazing what people miss, especially early morning, concentrating on getting to work, plus it's Sunday...And from the road, that's if he was seen at all, people might have thought he was cleaning the roof...And these days most people are busy texting instead of looking around them. Aren't they?'

'That's true,' Edna said from her corner. 'Sick to bloody death of people walking into me cos they're on them flaming phones. Saw a young lad nearly get run over the other day, and he carried on walking oblivious to the shocked driver, who by the way had to pull over...I mean the texting twit might have been totally in another world.'

'Texting twit!' Luke said.

'Aye.' Edna replied. That's what I call them, they haven't got a clue what's going on around them.'

'Think you just might have coined a new phrase, Edna.' Lorraine smiled.

'Happens all the time though you're right, in another world most of the kids today.' Carter added his agreement. 'I'm surprised there hasn't been a hell of a lot more accidents...Actually there probably have.'

'Yes okay, we get the picture.' Scottie looked skywards, then at Carter. 'Don't encourage her.'

But he was too late, Edna went on. 'You mark my words; in years to come people will have forgotten how to talk to each other. We'll have tiny little bodies, because we don't go anywhere or do anything, just stuck in a room with computers and phones and we'll have giant thumbs...Then because nobody ever meets up with anybody, we'll die out.' Edna nodded and turned back to her work.

Unable to contain himself at the picture in his head of the future human race with giant thumbs, and tiny bodies, Luke burst out laughing.

'For God's sake what have I just said, don't encourage her.' Scottie shook his head.

'Well,' Lorraine smiled. 'She does have a point.'

'Course I have.'

'And I know exactly just where to shove it,' Scottie muttered. Looking at Lorraine under his eyebrows and mouthing. 'You have no idea...Trust me, I bet anything you like, and she'll have got that idea out of one of those science fiction mags she's always reading. I swear she believes in little green men!'

'Do too.' Edna shrugged.

Only Lorraine had heard, them both, she smiled, knowing that really Scottie adored Edna, and would do anything for her. Looking away for a moment she bit down on her lip trying not to laugh.

'Right.' she said, composing herself as she looked down once more at the body of the young man, thinking, somewhere there is a family waiting for this son, husband, brother, father, to come home, torturing themselves every day, constantly wondering.

Is he alive?

Or is he dead?

Is he lying in some forgotten corner of a strange country, with no one to care.

Well. She vowed to herself. You will go home.

Was he sent to England to get money so that his family could eat, had he made regular payments to them, and were they already wondering why they hadn't heard from him? Inwardly she sighed, the ability of the human race to cause suffering to their own kind and others had always deeply upset her, but the things she had seen only strengthened her resolve to bring the culprits to justice. If only the fucking stupid do-gooders would do one. Lately the PC brigade had made their job just that bit harder. She thought, before saying. 'We'll get going then.Ring me the minute you get the DNA results Scottie.'

Scottie stepped back from the table as Sam came in and started to photograph the body. 'Yep, will do, my dear,' he said over his shoulder, to Lorraine.

A few minutes later with Lorraine driving, they were heading to the glass centre. Luke reached into the glove compartment and took out a pair of sun-glasses and handed them to Lorraine. 'Here I know you can't stand it too bright...Nothing worse than the spring sun in your eyes, is there?'

'Thanks,' she took the glasses and rubbed between her eyes before slipping them on. 'That's better, why the hell the sun is so sharp in the spring, beats me.'

'Well.' Carter started to say.

Lorraine held her left hand up. 'Save it Carter I don't really want to know.'

Luke looked over at her. 'Headache coming on?'

'Something like that.'

'There's some paracetamol in the glove compartment boss.' Carter said. 'I dropped them in the other day when I used your car. Me mother swears by them, she won't go anywhere without them, just in case.'

'Cheers.' Lorraine looked at Luke.

'Oh right,' Luke said after a moment as he began to rake through the contents of the glove compartment.

'There's a bottle of water in my bag.'

After Lorraine had swallowed the pills, Luke took the water from her and dropping it back into her bag, said 'That was pretty gruesome, as murders go.'

'Yes, it certainly was, especially the tearing off of the scalp, never knew that happened, must take some fucking strength to do that.'

'So if it takes longer to die that way...Then it looks like torture, you know making him suffer that much longer.'

'Or the perp has thought he was dead, turned his back for a moment, and the poor bugger did a runner.'

'More like a slow crawl from where ever he left the poor bastard for dead.'

In the back Carter said. 'That's what I think an' all boss. I think he dumped him in the river and somehow he got out. He could have crawled onto the roof hoping someone would see him, cos it would have been freezing in the river like Scottie said, you could live longer in the cold.'

Luke shrugged, mulling it over. 'Bloody long crawl though. I mean how many yards from the river to the Glass Centre?'

'Whatever, it looks like we've got another crazy bastard on the loose.' Lorraine muttered, as Luke again glanced sideways at her.

'I think there would have been signs if he'd been in the river. Don't you?' Luke said, as he turned his head to look out of the side window.

Carter nodded. 'Yeah, you're right, I'm sure all of his clothes were dry.'

'So, that rules the river out.'

'Well, we'll check it out in a mo.' Lorraine replied as they pulled up outside of the Glass Centre.

## CHAPTER TWENTY FIVE

Fiona, with Molly holding her hand tightly, because in the background they could still hear the little girl yelling at the top of her lungs even though she was now out of sight, and Oliver wearing a frown which looked in danger of becoming permanent, reached the shop. Puzzled as to why the girl had come running out of the shop, Fiona slowly opened the door. As they entered a woman screamed.

Fiona jumped in shock. 'What!'

'Mum.' Molly squealed. Frightened, she hid behind her mother. Shocked out of his frown Oliver glanced quickly at Fiona, and then down the aisle to where the scream had came from.

An oldish woman with thick streaks of gray in her long black hair was shaking her head and sobbing her eyes out, between screams she kept shouting over and over. 'No...No...No.' Quickly Fiona moved down the aisle, the woman looked at her and pointed towards the floor behind the counter. Fiona slipped Molly's hand into Oliver's. 'Stay here.'

Hurrying behind the counter Fiona gasped at the amount of

blood then got down and felt Mr Jansen's neck for a pulse, after a moment she looked up at Mrs Jansen. 'Have you phoned an ambulance...Or the police.'

Mrs Jansen shook her head. 'I...I only...I only just came down stairs....Is he...Is he?'

## CHAPTER TWENTY SIX

Kerry quickly showered then changed for work, a pair of red jeans and a black top, her clean tabard, navy with a red trim and the shops logo on it, was folded in her bag. Today's shift being a Sunday was twelve till four, and Gillian the manager was a stickler for time keeping.

Her phone lying on top of her bed, buzzed again. She stared at it as she chewed her bottom lip. There had been seven or eight messages since the original had arrived, she'd lost count, but each had said the same.

I'm watching you bitch.

Seriously creeped out, she was also very angry, and wishing she could physically strangle the phone.

Kerry picked the phone up, without looking at the screen and slipped it into the back pocket of her jeans. She'd decided not to tell her mother, who was sitting outside in the front garden where last night's unexpected high winds had caused havoc, with rubbish scattered everywhere. She was talking to old Mr Skillings, who last week had planted some yellow rose bushes for her.

Both of them were pleased that there had been no wind damage to the bushes. Enjoying some sun even though there was still a nip in the air, they were finishing off their cups of tea, and seriously wondering why ten minutes ago, Melanie Musgrove had run screaming up the street as if all the demons in hell were after her, and without breaking stride she'd run into her house.

Kerry knew that too much stress was not good for her mother and she'd only freak out if she knew about this phone rubbish. She also knew exactly what she would say. ''Just when things were finally going good for them, another creep has crawled out of the friggin woodwork.''

Although far from happy about the messages, Kerry was made of very stern stuff. 'I'll find out who you are, you cowardly bastard. And trust me I'll kick the fucking shit out of you,' she muttered under her breath, as she made her way downstairs and out into the garden. 'Don't think I won't, fucking creep.'

She stubbed her toe on the corner of the dustbin, yelled, then started to kick it.

'Bastard- bastard- bastard,' she muttered.

But for all of her brave talk she still felt a small twinge of nervousness. After all, she thought, she'd heard about these phone bullying or cyber bullying idiots, or whatever they wanted to call it. Just before she'd left school her friend had been stupid enough to put naked pictures of herself on the internet, which had gone viral, and she was still ashamed to come out of the house a couple of years later. Which was really a bit harsh for a mistake made by a kid, Kerry was thinking as she went out into the garden, glancing quickly up then down the street as her thoughts left her friends predicament and centered back on her own.

It could be anyone out there. A total stranger or even somebody I know...And that's what made it frightening, a whole different ball game than confronting people up front, this was the coward's way.

'Bastards!'

'Huh, who's talking to herself now?' Vanessa laughed.

'Morning my girl.' Mr Skillings waved his walking stick at her. 'Good run today?'

Kerry managed a quick smile and a nod in his direction, and ignoring her mother's comment, and still searching the street with her eyes, made her way to the gate.

Vanessa looked at Mr Skillings and gave a small shrug. 'See what I mean?'

'Teenagers,' he said. 'Up one minute down the next. They're all the same.'

'You got that right love. Try living with a whole flaming bunch of them.'

'Well, all I can say to that is, thank God that my own wallet munchers are now middle aged men, and finally starting to realise that they themselves are nowt but piggy banks.'

Vanessa grinned at Mr Skillings name for his kids, thinking that wallet munchers, was spot on, as Mr Skillings slowly rose to his feet.

'I'm off then pet, things to do bowling day up at the Welfare Hall with Doris and Dolly later on. And this time I'm gonna be the winner. You just watch,' he nodded his head with conviction. 'I'll show that pair the road home. You mark my words they won't know what's hit them today,' he winked at Vanessa. 'I've thrown the gauntlet down.'

'Okay, hope you do win. Anyhow, whichever way, enjoy. And again thank you for the roses.' Vanessa smiled.

About to say, my pleasure dear, Mr Skillings froze as an ambulance sirens blaring, came down the street.

'Hmm,' he said, as he sat back down. 'Best wait a bit, eh, see what this is all about.'

Vanessa nodded. 'It's all go this morning.'


Meanwhile as Kerry was getting off the bus outside of M and Co, in Houghton Le Spring's main street, her phone buzzed again. Gritting her teeth she did her best to ignore it as she crossed over the road to the paper shop where she worked. With a scowl on her face she walked past the other two girls behind the counter, they both looked at each other and frowned.

'Oh oh,' looks like it's gonna be a long day.'

The smaller of the two nodded. 'She's obviously in a lousy mood, pleased I'm off home at half twelve,' she glanced at her watch. 'Forty minutes give or take.'

'Lucky you.'

In the back of the shop and resisting the urge to scream Kerry took out her phone, there it was again the same message.

I'm watching you Bitch.

'For fucks sake!'

Quickly, after taking a moment to resist the urge to throw her phone against the wall, she texted back. "FUCK OFF." Only to receive a string full of smiley faces as a reply. For a moment she froze, as a feeling of white hot rage filled her. 'Cheeky bastard!'

Switching the phone off, and putting it in her pocket she went into the front shop. She knew that whoever it was, was nothing more than a creepy low life coward afraid to face people in real life, so they used phones and the internet to bully, and what was so annoying was the fact that she would probably never find out who the creep was, and the only way to get rid of the scumbag was a new fucking phone.

But how did he get my number?

Thought it was supposed to be private?

'Shit, didn't our Robbie lose his phone the other day? He's been searching every inch of the house since. Bet somebody's nicked it, and got my number.'

Walking onto the shop floor she began stacking cans of pop in the fridge, every now and then glancing into the street, she saw no one who looked as if they were watching her, an old man in a very long grey overcoat who she didn't know, and had never seen in Houghton before, stood across the road near to the bus stop he kept looking over into the shop then up the street but it was very obvious he was waiting for someone, besides she thought, he probably hasn't even got a phone and wouldn't know how to use one if he did.

Who the hell is the creep?

Frustrated, she gritted her teeth, and resisted the urge to take her phone out of her pocket and check again.

No, she thought, that's what he wants, me walking on eggshells, well he can fuck off.

'Can you pass me a can of Fanta please?'

Kerry jumped in shock and spun quickly round. A young man dark haired with hazel eyes, and who looked vaguely familiar was smiling at her. 'Sorry...What?'

'Can of Fanta, you're standing in front of them.'

Silently she handed him a can, he smiled and turned to walk away, then turned back. 'Do I know you?'

With a far from friendly tone, Kerry said. 'Dunno, do you?'

Shrugging, he stared at her for a moment before picking up a bar of chocolate, and moving to the counter.

Frowning, Kerry watched him walk out of the shop and cross the road. The old man was still standing there although he was now more leaning against the bus shelter, than actually standing.

Is it you? She wondered as the young man passed the old man without looking at him. Kerry watched until he was out of sight. Noting that he looked back at the shop more than once, she racked her brains knowing that he was familiar.

'Who the hell?'

## CHAPTER TWENTY SEVEN

Lorraine put the phone down. 'Alright guys, looks like Scottie was right, the dead man is certainly from Rumania.'

'Clever what they can do these days isn't it?' Sanderson said. 'Wish we'd had the technology thirty odd years ago. I know some right twats walking around today who should have been hanged and flaming well left to rot. Instead they're living a life of flaming luxury for their sins.'

Yeah, know one or two like that myself. Lorraine thought, but said. 'Anyhow he's sending some photos through, along with a set of finger prints, but my guess is he's an illegal and we won't be able to trace him.'

'So what the hell is he doing here? Dinwall asked.

Lorraine, Luke and Sanderson looked at him.

'Alright.' Dinwall shrugged, pulled a face and held his hands up, then more or less repeated what Sanderson had just said. When the others just kept on looking at him, he said again. 'Sorry...But Sanderson's right, high time they did bring the hanging back. If the public only knew some of the murdering sex creeps we have to deal with these days. Jesus!'

Not seeing Sanderson raising his eyebrows at him, but Dinwall realised he should not have mouthed off a few seconds later when Luke threw a file at him.

'Here make yourself busy and check up on these.'

Red-faced Dinwall picked up the file, muttering. 'Parking tickets,' to himself, as he went out the door.

'Really Luke, there was no need.' Lorraine snapped at him, while Sanderson also left the room.

'He's a thoughtless idiot.'

'Yes but he didn't mean anything by it.'

Luke shrugged and put his hand on Lorraine's shoulder, and seizing the moment said. 'Why can't you talk about it?'

Shrugging his hand off, she said. 'Because I don't fucking want to, alright. Why dredge it all up?'

'Because it hasn't gone away.'

Glaring at Luke she shook her head. 'Drop it I'm alright. How many times for God's sake.'

Luke sighed. It killed him to see her suffering, knowing there was nothing he could do about it, and once more hoping that soon the court case would end it all.

'Okay, I'll run the finger prints through the database.'

'Please,' standing Lorraine quickly slipped her jacket on. 'I've a meeting with Clark; it would be good to have a little more information on our man when I come back.'

'Yes.' Luke replied in the same prickly tone that Lorraine had used. Then he cursed under his breath, knowing she was suffering and he was behaving like a twat.

For a brief moment she paused on her way to the door, as Luke said. 'I'm sorry Lorraine I didn't mean for it to come out like that, truly I'm sorry.'

She looked at him. 'We'll talk later.' Then turning quickly she left the room.

'Damn.' Luke turned to his desk. All he wanted was his old Lorraine back.

## CHAPTER TWENTY EIGHT

'You are fucking kidding?' Jacko Musgrove said to his friend Danny Jordon, while Danny's cousin Len shook his head and looked gloomily at the floor. They were sitting on a bench, next to his leek trench in Len's allotment at Grasswell, supping a can of lager each. Danny and Len could not be more unlike if they were total strangers from different continents; quick to laugh Danny had a sense of humour, while his cousin Len looked as if he was in severe pain if he even managed to crack a smile.

'No way man.' Adam Glasier stared at Danny in amazement. The youngest of the gang with a mop of thick black hair, he shook his head in disbelief.

'That's what you said about our Santa gig isn't it and look how good that worked. Best Christmas we've had in years. Am I right guys?'

'Hmm, I suppose so.' Jacko said, remembering how happy Melanie and his mother had been. And it had been so good for once, to come out the other side of Christmas with no debt. A good few years since that had happened.

'Aye.' Adam replied. 'But this is down and out theft, you daft sod... And friggin dangerous.'

'Don't be bloody stupid.'

'I mean it.'

'And nowt else we've done isn't? Like when we went on the fag run, remember.'

'Like we're gonna forget that in a hurry,' Jacko said, flicking a spider off one of Len's newly planted cabbages. 'Chased about by what was practically the mafia, who put friggin drugs under the van, expecting sackless sods like us to carry them unknowingly across the friggin channel.'

'Aye, that's true.' Len mumbled.

They all nodded their heads as Jacko went on. 'And don't get me started on that friggin sheep fiasco, on Stanhope common.'

Adam burst out laughing, 'Now that was a blast.'

While Len coughed into his hand and said. 'Well. I wouldn't have called it that.'

Slowly Danny shook his head. 'You all enjoyed the fucking cash though, didn't youse?' He looked from one to the other, when no one replied, he went on. 'Anyhow, it's only a little bit of grass for Christ's sake. Not exactly the fucking crown jewels, is it. I mean for fucks sake?'

'Aye but it's somebody else's bit of grass, isn't it.' Jacko tutted and looked at the other two.

'Oh for fucks sake, are you lot in or out? It's not as if you're all exactly coming up with a plan, friggin' hell…Maybe's the lottery eh…Not a hope in hell's chance.'

'About that.' Len said.

'About fucking what?'

'The lottery.'

'Oh for fuck's sake Len, give it a rest.'

'Hmm…I don't know about that, he has a point, somebody's gotta win it, maybe's we should start a syndicate?' Adam nodded.

Danny shook his head. 'Can we get back to the point in question, for fuck's sake?'

'Okay, alright, but you're on about farmer Macintyre's grass and he's got a bloody big shotgun, evil old twat thinks he rules the world.' Adam said.

'How do you know that?' Len looked sideways at him.

'He, err…Never mind.'

About to say, all farmers have bloody shotguns, Danny kept quiet when Len dug him in his ribs.

Sensing a juicy bit of gossip, Len leaned forward. 'Go on man tell us.'

Adam tutted, before saying. 'No way!' But the other three just kept on staring at him, willing him to say more.

When the silence had stretched for a couple of minutes, which felt like forever to Adam, he said. 'Okay, Okay…You nosy bunch of nutters, if you friggin well have to know.' Taking a deep breath he hurried on. 'It was like this see, the mad twat chased me and a mate one night when we were out rabbiting.' Adam took a drink from his can, while the other three watched and waited for him to tell them more.

When he dragged the drinking out by taking another sup, the never patient Danny urged him on with a gentle punch in his back. 'Well, come on out with it, what happened?'

'Aye,' Len nodded eagerly. 'What he said.'

Seeing Adam's face go red they all leaned even further forward staring at him.

'Okay…Alright…You're like a set of fucking vultures,' Adam held his hands up, for a minute he stared back at them, then with a huge sigh he went on. 'The bastard caught up with us in the woods on the other side of Penshaw Monument, didn't he?'

'And?' Danny urged him on.

'Aye right. Six rabbits we had, that's all, one each for the pot the others to sell…'

'I do like a nice bit of rabbit.' Len smacked his lips. 'Nowt better, especially…'

Impatiently Danny shushed him and urged Adam on by

squeezing his arm and saying. 'More.'

Adam sighed, 'Alright, no need to get rough...Well anyhow he made us take all our clothes off, and me new shoes an' all, took the rabbits, the guns and all our gear and we had to walk home bollock fucking naked.'

Danny slapped the table with the palm of his hand as they all burst out laughing.

'Yeah thanks.' Adam curled his lip at them.

'So how did you get home?' Jacko asked, wiping his eyes as he stared at Adam.

'I just said, we fucking walked, how do you think?'

'Bollock naked!' Lens eyes were on stalks. 'You walked home bollock naked?'

'Bollock fucking naked.' Danny added.

Wide eyed Len shook his head.

Adam glared at Danny. 'It was nearly two o clock in the friggin morning, and we sort of crept home from house to house. Had a mini heart attack when we had to hide behind some stinking bins for half an hour, when a house party sort of spread out onto the street for a bit. Still got a scar on the side of me fucking knee where I knelt on some glass.'

This set them off laughing louder than before, so loud that the white and grey goat standing in the corner made a bolt for the shed, even Len was holding onto his stomach. 'Oh…I can just picture it. Oh my God,' he managed, gasping for breath.

After a few minutes when they finally calmed down, Danny said, 'Well guys, what do you all think then?'

Jacko adjusted his eye patch and sighed loudly. 'Is that all you can come up with?'

Danny nodded. 'At the mo…Yes.'

'I don't know, you haven't convinced me yet, it's a bit on the dodgy side mate.'

'Gotta plan?' Adam asked.

Shrugging his shoulders, Danny said. 'Sort of…I reckon… if we go about one o clock in the morning we can get a good haul in less than an hour, there are four of us. We can unload it all into Len's allotment then quick back for another load. Like I said, there are four of us, so it shouldn't take that long. Might even manage three or four runs, if we're lucky.'

'Yeah, lucky being the right word.' Adam said.

'How much grass has he got?' Len asked.

'A good few fields full,' Danny replied. 'Checked it out this morning as I was passing.'

'You could see it from the road? Len asked amazement in his voice and his raised eyebrows.

'Err, yes.'

'See what I mean,' Len looked from one to the other.' The rich get away with bloody murder. It's always the bloody same, you just name it.'

Cutting Len off from another rant, Jacko quickly asked. 'You got a buyer?'

'Well, I might have, gotta make one or two phone calls this afternoon like.'

'Might have!' Adam nearly choked on his drink. 'I'm not risking meeting up in the dark with that crazy fuck bastard ever again, for a might have sort of deal. For fucks sake no way man. Are you for fucking real, or what?''

Len frowned at him.

'It'll be good money, have you seen what the asking price for grass is these days?' Danny said.

They were all quiet for a moment then Jacko said. 'Well it's better than nowt I suppose, but a sort of, might have plan, not to keen on that like. You really need to come up with something better mate.'

'It will work, think about it. Besides you got anything better lined up?'

Jacko shook his head, he'd been at a loss ever since the market he'd worked on had folded a few years ago, blaming it on the rise in car boots. And the odd jaunts that Danny came up with certainly helped put food on the table.

Danny looked at the others. Slowly one by one they nodded.

'Okay, that's it, done deal. I'll pick you all up at midnight on the dot. Right?'

'No, best we make our way to yours you never know who's lurking about. I did tell you this the last time, if any body clocks the van outside of our houses that time of night they'll think we're up to something.' Jacko said.

'Yeah you're right. So tonight it is.' Danny downed his can. 'Right then, time I was off, gotta take the wife shopping.'

'Aye just when it's your turn to pop over the shop for some cans.' Len grumbled.

'I brought the beef sarnie's!'

'Aye to butter us up with, you slavery git,' Adam said. 'No change there man.'

'Whatever.'

'I'll have to be off as well. Told our Melanie I'd take her and her mate to Hetton baths...And my mother's going bowling with her little gang.'

'Now that should be good to watch, the three of them can barely bend to fasten their shoe laces.' Adam laughed.

'You're a cheeky bastard.' Jacko stared at Adam.

'Sorry...Sorry I was just saying like. Didn't mean no harm.'

'Yeah well watch your mouth in future.'

'Alright guys, let's not fall out.' Danny hastily added. He knew his friend Jacko had been a bit edgy of late ever since he'd beaten a lad up for bothering his kid, plus his girlfriend Christina had somehow disappeared. And that was fairly bugging him.

'I'm sorry, really didn't mean any harm mate, you know that.' Adam said again.

Jacko nodded. 'Okay, sorry for snapping, just think in future before you put your big gob into gear.'

'I will-I will.'

'Now that's impossible.' Len muttered as Jacko and Danny left them.

'He's been fucking tetchy ever since he had that run in with that fucking Dev creature a few months back. And he's fretting over his lass Christina, she's obviously had enough of him and pissed off, only he can't see it.' Adam finished his can and threw it into the bin.

'Aye your right, he has an' all. Not like Jacko at all though is it. But that last comment.' Len raised his eyebrows and shook his head as he went on. 'Best not let him hear you say that if I were you, cos I'm not scraping you up off the road mate.'

Adam gulped. 'Guess you're right.'

Len nodded as he finished his own drink and placed the can

exactly in the centre of the bench making sure that there was exactly the same amount of round knot mark showing around the bottom of the can, watching him Adam shook his head.

Len checked his shoelaces, 'Well gotta look up some more seed prices.'

'What the hell for, it's not exactly a market garden you've got here, it's probably the smallest allotment around.'

Len shrugged, 'It's mine though.'

Adam snapped his fingers. 'Just had a great idea, why don't you grow the grass?'

Len's jaw dropped in amazement. 'Me! No way.'

'Come on man, we could make a small fortune.'

'Get lost.'

Grinning behind Len's back. Adam headed for home.

## CHAPTER TWENTY NINE

They say when you are drowning your whole life flashes right in front of you, for the last six hours his life had not flashed but took a slow tortures walk right up to the present.

He knew what the sounds had been now, earth hitting the top of a coffin. He had been to enough funerals this past year to know what the sound was like.

That's all it could have been.

His coffin.

He shivered at the very thought of it, his tears had long dried up as he wondered again, how long a man could live without water.

A week?

Five days?

Four days?

Two days?

He tried to wriggle his toes in the tiny cramped space, his legs burned with pain, from his hips to his toes his whole body ached for the sheer luxury to simply be able to stretch, more than anything in the world.

The tears he thought were all dried up suddenly ran down his face again, he tried as hard as he could stretching his tongue to its limits to claim the moisture. But they were out of reach.

Oh, yes, he suddenly thought, lifting his hand he used his middle finger to wipe as much of the moisture from his face that he could, and sucked on his finger,

It barely wet his lips.

## CHAPTER THIRTY

Vanessa left Mr Skillings sitting in the garden for a minute, while she went inside and phoned the Beehive, checking for the third time since she had booked, that everything was fine for Robbie's surprise birthday party; assured again that yes everything was good to go, she put the phone down and leaned against the wall. Her heart was singing, she took a deep breath and held onto the top of the chair to stop herself from dancing. She couldn't believe that for once in her life, everything was running smoothly.

In fact, she thought, it's going too smoothly; something has gotta go wrong.

She had given up all thoughts of a normal life years ago, to people like her, normal just didn't happen. Jinxed from birth, that's what she'd been, and there was nothing she could do about it never mind Sandra saying she had to keep positive and get rid of all negative thoughts. For a moment her mood slipped.

Stop it. She told herself. Sandra is right!

Going into the kitchen and forgetting all about Mr Skillings, she started peeling the vegetables for the Sunday dinner which would be at tea time this week, as both Robbie and Kerry were at work.

Work, she thought, her mood rising again, two kids at work, two of my kids. She dashed a proud tear out of her eye. 'Who would have thought it eh?' She muttered, as another tear ran down her face.

And not only working, but Kerry to run for England. She pictured herself and her family watching Kerry lift the trophy on high and her heart swelled with pride. And Darren, she hugged herself. Darren and his football, his teacher had such high hopes for him. Circumstances had spoiled his last chance, but she knew there would be others, he was so good. There was time, plenty of time for Darren to live his dream.

So much to live for now.

Sandra is right. Think positive.

Just a year and a half and so much has changed for the better. None of them, not even Sandra had known just how close she had been to taking an overdose and ending all of the fucking misery. Twice she'd held the bottle of pills in her hand, wishing for this terrible existence to end, twice she'd put the bottle back in the drawer knowing deep inside if there was ever to be a third time, then that would be it.

'Don't go there.' She whispered.

'Never go back.'

'Every day is a new day.'

Suddenly remembering Mr Skillings, she said. 'Shit!'

Grinning to herself, she abandoning the turnip and carrots and moved to the bench where she plugged the kettle in, and got some fresh cups from the cupboard.

A few minutes later, a smile firmly in place she went back to Mr Skillings with another cup of tea for them both.

## CHAPTER THIRTY ONE

Dinwall pulled up outside of the police station in Morpeth, he loosened his seatbelt, switched the engine off, and was about to open the door when Sanderson made a great show of heaving a massive sigh of relief.

'Oh for God's sake if you've got something to say, just fucking well spit it out will you...Your amateur dramatics are crap and you've been nowt but a pain in the friggin arse, since the beginning of the year.'

Leaning over and snatching the keys out of the ignition Sanderson glared at Dinwall. 'Right, seeing as you're asking, you my friend are one flaming crap driver, in fact one of the worst I've ever encountered...Your name should be Speed not Dinwall. That alright with you?'

'And yours should flaming well be Snail. Okay. Is that alright with you?'

Sanderson shrugged, as Dinwall went on. 'And...What's the flaming point in driving a police car if you aren't going to use all the friggin equipment that comes with it to get through the fucking lousy traffic?'

Sanderson shrugged again, and got out of the car. They reached the door of the station together. Dinwall slightly bigger than Sanderson managed to grab the handle first and with a sarcastic smile, ushered Sanderson inside. 'After you.'

'Clever sod.' Sanderson muttered.

They showed the desk sergeant their badges, he nodded. 'Right guys, been expecting you, next couple of minutes, and they'll be here with him. Take a seat over there.' He gestured with his hand towards a bench at the far pale green painted wall, where a local drunk was sitting on a bench with his head in his hands.

They walked over and seeing Dinwall about to speak to the drunk, the sergeant shook his head and raised his finger to his mouth. He had barely finished the gesture when the side door opened and the smallest policewoman Dinwall and Sanderson had ever seen, walked in followed by a tall thin policeman, and a man mountain.

'Bloody hell. Have you ever in your life seen anyone so big?' Sanderson muttered, as Dinwall shook his head in disbelief at the sheer size of the man.

'Hello there.' The woman police officer, a very pretty young woman with short blonde hair, quickly stepped forward and introduced herself. 'I'm PC Helen Darby. You must be Dinwall and you Sanderson. And,' she gestured to the policeman. 'This is PC Davidson.' The tall officer standing next to her silently looked from one to the other and gave each a small nod.

'The other way round.' Sanderson smiled.

'Sorry?'

Dinwall nodded. 'Yes, you got it mixed up. I'm Dinwall. He's Sanderson.'

'His pony tail is better than yours.' Sanderson muttered, looking at Grossmont. 'So much better.'

Then still looking at the man they had come to collect, he thought. Hope I never meet this bugger in a dark alley, he's gotta be the biggest guy in England.

Ignoring Sanderson's quip in his ear, Dinwall said to PC Darby. 'Shouldn't he be cuffed?'

For once agreeing with something Dinwall had said. Sanderson quickly nodded.

PC Darby turned and looked up at the silent man. 'You don't need handcuffs do you Alfie?'

Alfie smiled down at her and shook his head. She turned back to Dinwall. 'I assure you he'll be peaceful. He also has an alibi for the time of the murder.'

Not really entirely convinced, about her first sentence. Dinwall said, scratching the side of his nose. 'Okay if you say so. But our orders are to bring him back with us.'

PC Darby stepped to one side. 'Fine, he's all yours. See you soon Alfie.'

Dinwall reached for the man's arm to lead him to the car while Sanderson completed the paperwork with the desk sergeant.

Forty five minutes of complete silence later, they pulled up outside of Houghton police station.

Sanderson, who still had the car keys in his possession had pulled rank, and insisted on driving home, said. 'Take him in while park round the back.'

Dinwall shrugged, and took the silent suspect into the station. After signing him in, he led him towards an interview room on the ground floor.

'Just sit there, we'll be back to interview you shortly.'

Mr Grossmont nodded amiably, and sat down.

For a moment Dinwall watched him through the glass door, the man hardly moved and just sat staring ahead of him. When he walked into the office a few minutes later, Lorraine, Luke and Sanderson were standing by the window.

'Sanderson doesn't seem to think that Alfie Grossmont has anything to do with it, what about you?' Lorraine asked as he walked towards them.

'Pretty much the same boss, he actually hasn't said a word since we picked him up. But also, Morpeth don't seem to think it's him either. In fact PC Darby actually seemed,' he shrugged. 'Quite fond of him.'

'Right then, let's find out, err, not you Dinwall, you still have some parking fines to sort.'

Barely managing to stop himself from growling at the grin on Sanderson's face, Dinwall muttered, 'Yes boss,' as he made his way out of the room.

## CHAPTER THIRTY TWO

Mr Skillings still hadn't left Vanessa's garden, there was far too much going on, and they were yet to find out why Melanie Musgrove had come screaming up the street, yelling for her dad, nor why just two minutes ago an ambulance, lights flashing and alarms blaring, had gone haring past them in the general direction of the shop.

Standing at the gate, Mr Skillings was wondering if he should go over and see Doris about what was wrong with Melanie, because there was definitely something amiss with the bairn. I just hope it's not that Dev again, I saw him creeping around earlier. He rested on his cane for a moment, and spotted Dolly Smith from the corner house heading towards them. Turning to Vanessa he said. 'Here's Dolly, she might know something.'

'Well if she doesn't, nobody will. And that's a fact.' She grinned at Mr Skillings.

Just before Dolly reached them and about to step onto the road to cross over a police car flew past, lights flashing in competition with the ambulance.

'Friggin hell, what's going on?' Vanessa said. 'It's looking like Blackpool illuminations.'

'You heard anything dear?' Mr Skillings stepped back, and looked at Dolly as she opened the small gate.

'That's just what I was wondering as well…' Dolly said, as she reached them.

'So you don't know?'

Dolly shook her head at Vanessa.

'Well we don't either.' Mr Skillings turned to Vanessa. 'Youse two girls need anything from the shop?'

Vanessa jumped up as Dolly nodded. 'I'll just tell our Claire to watch the others while I'm gone, lazy buggers are still lying in bed, playing on them daft computer games, and I need some more potatoes for the dinner.'

'Not good for them.' Mr Skillings said.

'What potatoes?' Dolly smiled at Vanessa.

'Very funny, you know what I mean.'

Together they headed up the street, turning the corner and passing the swings, they saw the ambulance and the police car, parked outside of the shop.

'Shit.' Vanessa said. 'Hope it's not Mrs Jansen, she's been a bit poorly lately. Wasn't she waiting for some tests coming back, you know from when she fell and hurt her hip in that bit of snow ve had just after Christmas?'

Mr Skillings nodded. 'Aye she has that, been waiting ages, poor bugger's been through the mill and back.'

'Don't think it's her mind you, she's getting into the back of he ambulance but she looks fine to me...But it still might be her. Because you never can tell can you?' Dolly nodded in the direction of the ambulance.

'Isn't that my new neighbour?' Mr Skillings asked, staring at a woman, as they drew closer. 'I'm sure it's her, I did smile when he came down the path, but she seemed to look right through me as if I wasn't even there.'

Looking at the young woman standing near the shop doorway alking to a policeman, with a couple of kids in tow, Vanessa shrugged. 'Not sure, only just caught the back of her when they went down the path. Knocked me bloody shin on the table didn't I rying to get a better look.'

'That'll teach you to be nosy.' Dolly said.

'You what?' Vanessa laughed

'Hmm,' Mr Skillings suppressed a grin. 'Guess I had a better ook than you did, they were with that young ginger copper, all dressed up in a suit as if he was pretending not to be a copper...Yes definitely' think it's her.'

They joined a couple of other neighbours; that was when they found out that it was definitely Mr Jansen who had been carried into the ambulance, and not his wife.

Slowly and quietly the ambulance pulled away from the shop.

'Well, that doesn't look good.' Mr Skillings said, a few of the neighbours nodded their heads.

'What do you mean?' Vanessa asked.

Mr Skillings looked at her, for a moment he was unsure what to say, he knew that Mr Jansen over the years had been very kind to Vanessa helping her out in more than one hour of need, even though at odd times under the influence she had much maligned him, when he'd refused to serve her any more drink.

'Well...Because...Because Vanessa pet...It's in no hurry to get where it's going.'

'Shit...You mean?' Vanessa looked from Dolly to Mr Skillings as the penny slowly dropped.

## CHAPTER THIRTY THREE

In her bedroom Melanie quickly moved her pile of favourite books onto the floor, and two of the seven porcelain dolls she loved to collect, away from the windowsill, her collection of assorted cuddly toys were thrown hastily onto her bed. She used two piles of her books to stand on, and pushing the pink checked curtains to one side, she craned her neck to look out of the bedroom window. But she could only see a few people going in the direction of the shop- of the shop its self she could only see the end of the cream painted wall, and that was with squashing her cheek hard against the window. She contemplated opening the window and popping her head out, only she was frightened in case Dev was still hanging around.

After Melanie had told her anxious grandmother what she had seen in the shop, Doris had phoned for an ambulance before taking Melanie's hand to go over and tell her friends, because Mr Skillings knew first aid, then to hurry down to the shop with him, only Melanie had refused to go with her and had ran up stairs. Doris was torn in two, her instincts screaming at her to go and see if she could help, her heart demanding that she stay with Melanie. Hearing the ambulance go past was a relief, they would get there before she ever could.

Wondering if there was something her granddaughter was not telling her, because Melanie was acting very strange; and anxious to find out just what really had gone on, Doris was now standing at the bottom of the stairs, her arms folded across her chest and shouting for Melanie to come back down.

Moving to her bed and sitting on the edge, Melanie tried to stop her limbs from trembling.

After a moment she took a deep breath and shouted. 'No nana, I don't want to...You go...Just go...I'll be alright.' She tried as hard as she could to keep the tremor out of her voice. But Doris was not so easily fooled.

Doris was right to suspect that Melanie was not telling her everything. Melanie had left out the fact that Dev was the last person she had seen coming out of the shop not only that, she had omitted to tell Doris that Dev was even there.

The last thing she wanted was for her dad to fight with Dev again. She was still struggling to get the image out of her mind and feared it would never go away.

'Melanie, get yourself down here now and tell me just what the hell is going on with you.' Doris demanded.

'Don't want too.'

'Melanie.'

'Nana!'

'Now.'

Heaving a great sigh, Melanie left her bedroom and slowly walked down the stairs.

'Do you think Mr Jensen's alright nana?' she asked as she reached the bottom of the stairs.

Doris folded her arms across her chest and ignoring Melanie's question said. 'There's something you're not telling me girl...I know there is...Come on out with it.'

Melanie put her head down. 'No nana.'

'What?'

'No nana.' Melanie repeated.

'Come again girl.'

Melanie sighed and looked at Doris. 'I don't want dad to find out. Cos, cos he might...No nana, it, it's nothing. Honest...It's nothing nana.'

'Find out what, come on Melanie, you aren't making much sense, bloody hell. It's like pulling teeth.'

'Nothing nana.'

'Just tell me girl...If some thing's bothering you then I need to know; now.' Doris folded her arms even tighter across her chest.

'Out with it Melanie or you'll be grounded for a month.'

'A month!' Melanie gulped. Then quickly shook her head. 'It's nothing nana, just got a head ache...Honest.'

And the band played believe it if you like! Doris thought, staring in frustration at her granddaughter.

'A month's not fair nana, not for having a headache, is it?'

'Don't try and wheedle your way out of it Madam, I wasn't born yesterday.'

## CHAPTER THIRTY FOUR

After picking the still sobbing woman up out of the gutter and helping her to the door, Dev left her, and refusing her invitation, between sobs to come inside, which actually turned into begging, he started to walk away. He threw his empty milk bottle, which he's picked back up in case the crazy Arun came back and started on him, over the next garden wall as he left her yard and headed up the Burnside towards Houghton town centre. Totally unaware of what was going on at the shop only a few streets away.

The sound of glass breaking brought a smile to his face, which quickly left a moment later when he heard. 'Hey, what the hell do you think you're doing creep?' A deep voice yelled at him. 'Come back here and pick this up, before I make mincemeat out of you, stupid twat.'

'No way.' Dev muttered.

The owner of the voice was hidden by a large tree, but guessing that it was a bloke and possibly a big one, Dev legged it up the street. Reaching the town centre he paused a moment outside of the new bike shop. He had always wanted a bike, but never asked again, as the first time he asked, resulted in a black eye when he was eight, which had not been the first, nor the last. Even then he should have known better, but just about everyone he knew had a bike. Even Tom, who also sported the odd black eye, the competition between them to find an excuse for the bruise's went to extremes the older they got. Even to more than once telling their teachers that they had been fighting with each other.

Wonder where Tom is now? He wondered briefly as other memories flooded in.

Another friend used to give him a backer and sometimes, well once or twice he let him ride his bike, but it had never been enough. It was the same with the sledges when the snow came just about everyone had them as well, while all he had was a big black plastic sack, or a dirty carrier bag, as did Tom, no bike or sledge there either. That was of course, the odd time he'd managed to sneak out. He still had scars on his bottom where ice and stone had ripped through the bags.

He looked at the back of his hand, a small burn scar from the first time he had tried to boil an egg at seven years old, the only thing in the house to eat, both the boiling water and the egg had ended up on the floor. There was a matching scar, only much larger on his right shin. But that was from a different time, a year later when he'd tried to run away, from yet another drunken stranger brought willingly into the house.

His body shook, he could actually feel the boiling water hitting him and burning into his skin, he could see the egg rolling across the floor and crashing into the washer, where undercooked it lay in a watery mess. The dried in stain had still been there years later when freedom had finally happened.

There were other scars, scars that he could not account for. He had no memory of how they had come about, and guessed they must have happened when he'd been little more than a toddler. Or the reason for the scar had been so terrible he had blocked it.

With a growl he gritted his teeth, moved on and started the business of wrapping the memories up again. One by one, as each memory faded for the moment, the wetness in his eyes dried.

To get his thoughts going in the right direction he took out his phone and began texting as he walked.

A moment later he pressed send with another smile on his face.

## CHAPTER THIRTY FIVE

Unaware that he had just missed Dev by a few minutes, Jacko walked up the street to his house, hands in the pockets of his black leather jacket. He nodded at a few neighbours on the other side of the street as he passed, deep in conversation as they were it was only Lucy Brockenfield who noticed him, she gave him a wave and a smile, but moving on Jacko was once again preoccupied with his thoughts.

Where the hell are you Christina? He wondered, yet again.

Why did you just disappear like that?

Really thought we had something going.

Why did you just disappear like that?

He shook his head in frustration as he looked over at her father's house, it had a kind of dead look to it, the old man had always been a sort of recluse, but even more so these days. He'd begged him to inform the police about Christina's disappearance shortly after Christmas, the old fool had refused, stating that Christina was an adult and there was nothing they could do. He had been right, this Jacko had found out when angry and frustrated he had told the police himself.

The police had gone through the motions even searched her father's house but as there were no suspicious circumstances, there was virtually nothing for them to go on.

So, Christina had joined the ranks of the two hundred thousand people that go missing for whatever reason in the UK each year. Most of them turning up within forty-eight hours but a substantial lot are never heard of again. So he'd been told by Lorraine Hunt one morning when he had seen her walking her dog down the beck. What he'd wanted to know at the time was, where the hell did the substantial lot go to. And for that, she had told him, there was no answer. Except that if someone wanted to stay missing, then there was very little anyone could do. She had however ordered the search of her father's house, and for this he had been very grateful.

But Jacko knew that Christina was not the sort of person to just up sticks and take off for no reason. At least that's what he had thought- until her father much on the defensive told him that this was certainly not the first time that Christina had gone walk about, in fact it was at least three times he'd said, but she'd always turned up within the month. What he hadn't said, but what Jacko guessed rightly, was that each time she'd gone had been after a row with the miserable old bastard.

He'd took it upon himself to get leaflets with her picture on printed, and hand them out asking if anyone had seen her. From Sunderland to Newcastle, to Durham to Middlesbrough, and many towns in between. He'd trawled the streets handing them out, not one single person amongst the ones that had stopped and given him a moment of their time, remembered seeing her.

And now nearly four months into the New Year, he was no further forward and seriously missing the love of his life and the thought that he had just about done everything he could think of to find her, and there was nothing else he could do, had led to many sleepless nights and filled him with frustration, which tortured the life out of him.

What the hell else can I do?

His head hurt with the helplessness of it all.

With a sigh he opened the gate and walked down the steps to the front door.

'Just tatty pot for dinner today son, gotta save me energy to beat those two daft old buggers at bowls this afternoon. Be ready in five.' Doris said as he walked into the kitchen.

'Aye, can't have the motley crew beating you, eh mam.' He replied with a smile he didn't feel.

'No chance.'

Shoving her reading glasses to the top of her head, Doris turned back to washing the dishes, as Jacko grabbed a ginger snap biscuit from the biscuit tin then went into the sitting room where he flopped in front of the television and picked his newspaper up.

Doris was worried about Jacko, even though he constantly snacked on biscuits, his weight had dropped recently and he just didn't have his usual zest, when he wasn't in the pub he was stuck in front of the telly all day. At least he seemed to have some kind of hope when he was dishing his leaflets out, but now it was as if he'd just given up.

She wished now that he'd never got it off with Christina, nice girl though she was, at first she'd been happy for them they were good together. When he'd finally got rid of that moron Melanie's mother, he'd been settled and quite content with the life he had. And Christina had made his contentment complete. But losing his market stall had unsettled him a bit. But Christina going missing had unsettled him a lot.

And now- how the hell to tell him of the latest problem? She had got nothing out of Melanie, which didn't necessarily mean there was nothing; the kid could be as stubborn as a mule at the best of times, just like her bloody father, cos Jacko's got a stubborn streak a mile long.

God only knows where they get it from!

She shook her head. Kids! Doesn't matter how old they get, you still worry about them.

Putting his newspaper down, Jacko picked the remote up, flicked through the channels and settled on a replay of Top Gear.

Ten minutes later Doris appeared at the sitting room door drying her hands on a lemon and white checked tea-towel. 'Madam is up stairs son. Something's up with the little minx, more than what's gone on along the shop, but it's like pulling teeth trying to get anything out of her.'

'What's gone on at the shop like?'

'Didn't I say?'

Jacko shook his head.

'Well, according to Dolly and Mr Skillings, and Vanessa, who got it from Mr and Mrs Tonville, there's only just been a murder up at the bloody shop.'

'What?'

'Aye. Phoned for an ambulance, cos it was our Melanie what found him, but didn't like to leave the bairn on her own.'

'What?'

Shit! Now I've gone and dropped the bairn right in it.

## CHAPTER THIRTY SIX

After telling the police everything she had seen in the shop and around the shop, which was really very little. Fiona had taken her children up to the co-op store in Houghton. Quite impressed by the array of food available, she stocked up.

Back home, and pleased she had something to occupy her mind with, she left a chicken out to defrost and opened a couple of cans of tomato soup, a nice brown roll each that would do for lunch, thank fully the kids loved it, and the main meal with plenty of veg, would be later.

Soup on the boil, Fiona took out her phone and rang her husband again, the kids were in the garden so she let it ring and ring. 'Damn where the hell are you. For fuck's sake?' She slammed her fist down on the bench.

She tried her brother's number. No answer.

'Where the hell?' She sighed. She was starting to feel all alone, and frightened. It seemed like she had been deserted by her husband, and Stella.

She stared out of the window as she chewed on her thumb nail a habit she hated in others. I'm kidding myself, I am alone and frightened.

Something has happened!

I know it has.

'Where the hell?' It took some determination for her not to stamp her foot in frustration, like Molly.

'Mum.' Molly said from the doorway startling her. 'Can me and Ollie go down to the swings?'

Fiona sighed. The last thing she wanted was for her children to think they were prisoners, but she had to be careful.

Why couldn't we have been somewhere else that night?

Why was it us that had to see it?

Why didn't we turn right instead of left?

'Mum!' This time it was Oliver.'

'Sorry.' Fiona shook herself. 'Course you can, but make sure you stay with your sister Oliver...And Molly it is, may Oliver and I. Not Oliver and me. How many times?'

Oliver nodded solemnly as Molly turned her nose up and walked out of the room.

'Oh,' Fiona shouted after them. 'And don't go mixing with any of the local riff raff.'

Oliver stopped and turned round, his left eyebrow raised, he asked. 'Does that rule apply when we go to the local school?'

For a moment Fiona froze. 'I didn't mean...'

'Face it mother, you're a snob.'

Without waiting for her to answer Oliver pushed Molly in front of him and the headed outside.

She watched them go without answering her son as they both set off down the street towards the swing park. Her hands clenched as her whole body was wracked with anxiety. As well as everything else that was going on she feared that Molly *was* turning into a common street kid, she was certainly starting to sound like one. And that was after a couple of weeks mixing with them. The last school had been a disaster, and the teacher had tried to put all the blame on Molly saying that she was not a good mixer and she spent most of her time bragging.

Molly would not do that.

'And I'm not a snob,' she muttered. 'And I only want what's best for them.'

Biting back a sob, she turned and picking up their bags went up stairs to the bedrooms. She started on the room that was to be Molly's-as she unwrapped the picture of her daughter sitting on her father's knee in Disney Land Florida two years ago, with her and Oliver standing at each side, slowly she ran her finger over her husband's face.

'Why?' With a heavy sigh she placed the picture on the stand next to the single bed and once more blinked back the tears.

'Why, oh why did you have to do the right thing?' she muttered. 'You could have walked away.'

'You should have walked away.'

'Everything you ever worked for thrown away, playing the fucking hero.'

'Damn you!' she punched the pillow in frustration before burying her head in it and sobbing loudly.

## CHAPTER THIRTY SEVEN

The young woman scrubbed as hard as she could at the bench where the blood had slowly and steadily dripped from the latest scalp hanging above it, there were six in all each one a permanent threat of what would happen if you ever tried to escape from this living hell, although some-unable to bare it any longer took the chance and paid the price.

Two black, two blonde, and one ginger. And one, one that only had greying tufts clinging stubbornly to the skin. She paused for a moment as she blinked a tear from her eye.

Ginger, no one had ever known her real name, had been here when she herself had arrived. They had been friends and prisoners in this place, until Ginger having reached as far as she could go and knowing what the result would be, had slapped a punter and tried to do a runner.

She glanced once more at the scalp, a few shades lighter than her own auburn hair and wondered if she would ever get out of this living hell, and wishing for the millionth time that she herself, had never stormed out of the house that night. Another row at home, a boyfriend that was too busy trying to make money, and she'd fallen right into the trap of someone being nice to her.

And then panicked because things were going too fast, and frightened that at last she had found someone who loved her and even more frightened in case it did not work out.

And so she had ran, confused angry at her boyfriend and her father, right into the arms of a stranger.

What the hell had possessed her to go back to his flat?

I'm not that sort of girl never had been.

Fool…Fool…Fool. That's all I am!

She stamped her foot in frustration, then quickly looked at the door, held her breath for a moment, when it didn't open she let the air out of her lungs and with a shake of her head, turned back to her scrubbing.

Although, she thought, as she gazed at the scalps again, she wondered as she did most days, if the owners weren't better off than those still held here.

## CHAPTER THIRTY EIGHT

Suzy Lumsdon was sitting by herself on one of the swings in the park; holding on to the chain with one hand, with the other she was busy pulling out the plaits that her sister Claire had insisted on putting in her hair, even though she had told Claire that she hated them. But Claire never listened.

She was about to move over to the slide, when a girl of around her own age accompanied by an older boy walked over to the swings. The girl, after looking Suzy up and down with a sneer sat on the swing next to her while the boy, went and sat on one of the wooden seats dotted around the park. Putting his ear plugs in and switching his mobile on, he became oblivious to the world.

Suzy smiled at the girl, but when the girl stuck her tongue out at her, Suzy quickly looked the other way.

Not taking kindly to being ignored, Molly snapped. 'I'm Molly, what's your name...And aren't you that little scruff who was staring in our window a while ago?'

'No.'

'Yes you were.'

'Was not.'

Suzy turned and stared at her. 'And I'm not a scruff; I'm Suzy...S U Z Y...Not S U S I E... And you're, very very cheeky. And I was not staring in the window, it wasn't me-that was our Emma. And you are right nasty...And it's a good job our Emma isn't here, cos she'd tell you off. She might even pull your hair.'

Molly snorted at her. 'No I'm not nasty, you don't even know me, so how can you say that? And what's so special about this Emma thing?'

Suzy shrugged. 'You don't want to find out.'

'Bothered! Anyhow, how much was that dress then?'

Not having a clue, nor a care how much her dress was, Suzy shrugged again, this time a long drawn out exaggerated shrug that started way down in her body.

'Mine was sixty five pounds, that's not far off one hundred pounds is it... It's a designer dress...From the best shop in London.' She tossed her head. 'So are my shoes,' she looked at Suzy's scuffed trainers, and turned her nose up. 'Bet they are off a cheap market stall.'

Again Suzy gave her exaggerated shrug. 'It's forty pounds off a hundred and that's nearly half, so there. Maybe you should learn to count.'

'We have a swimming pool at my house...Bet you don't have

one, do you?'

'Err...No.'

'And we have a cinema room where we can watch all the best films...Oh, I so hate it here. I swim every day at home, that's when I'm not riding my pony.'

Deciding that she did not like the new girl very much, and knowing that her sister Emma would have called her a posh cow, and probably knocked her off her swing. Suzy rose up from her swing.

'Are you leaving?'

'Aye.'

Molly frowned. 'Why?'

'Cos you're a stuck up cow-snob.'

'Am not.'

'Aye but you are.'

'Hu, you don't even know me.'

'Don't want too.' Suzy turned to go.

'Don't go.'

'Why?' She turned back and looked at her.

Molly shrugged. 'Because.'

'Because what?'

'I want someone to play with.'

'But all you do is brag about swimming pools and pony's.'

Suzy flicked her hair off her shoulders the way she had seen Emma do. 'Bye.'

Molly looked down at her designer shoes and sighed. 'I'm sorry.' she muttered. 'Don't go.'

Looking at her, Suzy sat back down. 'Okay.' She said after a moment.

Molly brightened up. 'Do you go to that school along the road, the one with the big red painted doors?'

Suzy kicked at the gravel with her right foot. 'What for?'

'Well because I am starting there tomorrow, most probably in your form. The last year?'

'That's our Emma's year.'

'Do they have computers?'

'Yes. On a Friday morning for us.'

'Just one lesson a week?'

'Aye. But I think your year has more.'

'That's shocking, what sort of dump is it?'

'It's not a dump...I like it. My teacher, Miss Martin is very nice, to everybody.'

Molly looked Suzy up and down. 'Well you would say that, wouldn't you?'

Suzy threw her a puzzled look.

'You don't know any better cos you're common folk. That's

what my aunt say's and she's always right. She knows some real princesses.'

'Real ones?' Suzy asked, wide eyed.

Molly nodded, then slumped in her swing. A moment later she sat up and smiled at Suzy. 'Have you got a phone?'

'No, mam says I might get one not this Christmas coming but the next one, cos it's our Emma's turn to get one before me, that's if I'm good. Have you got one?'

Molly pulled a face. 'Mum took it away, just got it the other week, because my other one fell in the pool.'

'Why did she take it away?'

'Because it can be, err... traced, that's right...she said,' standing up she stamped her foot. 'I so hate it here.'

'Why would it be traced?'

'Can't tell.'

'Why?'

'Because for.' She sat back down and started to swing. After a moment Suzy joined her.

When they had slowed down, Suzy looked at Molly, and asked. 'So why are you here?'

Molly glanced over at her brother who was staring straight ahead of him. Then she whispered. 'Because we're all on the run from them.' She nodded solemnly.

Suzy frowned her puzzlement. 'On the run?'

Again Molly nodded solemnly.

'Who's them?'

'Don't know, something dad and my uncle saw. I just heard them talking to mum, dad and uncle I mean, not them. They don't think I know, but I do cos I heard everything.'

'Why do you call her mum?'

Molly shrugged, 'Don't know, just do. Why do you call your mum, mam?'

Both girls started giggling.

## CHAPTER THIRTY NINE

The talk in the Blue Lion that afternoon was all about the murder of the shop keeper in the Seahills shop.

'Apparently,' Dick Grimes said to his mates between the regulars doing their karaoke singing as they sat round a table. 'The poor old bugger had his head kicked in. Really badly an 'all, and they robbed the till, took hundreds of pounds, the whole weeks takings, so I heard.'

'Aye that's what I heard as well.' Jimmy Carrolls chimed in, as he ran his fingers over his dark beard. 'Reckon there was blood all over the place. Decent bloke he was, damn shame. Also they reckon there was definitely more than one. Fucking cowards, that's what they are.'

The other three men nodded, as Dick said. 'Aye, you're not safe no where these days man. Just read the papers and our lass is terrified to turn the telly on most mornings these days, the news is that bad either from around the world, or in your own bloody street... Fucking frightening isn't it?' He looked around at his friends, who all nodded again, just as the Karaoke started and stopped any attempt at a conversation, as one of the regulars belted out the old Eagles hit. ''*Hotel California.*''

A minute later the door opened and Dev walked in, immediately Mrs Archer, wearing a sickly lime green dress, which did nothing for her pale colouring, and made her look even more like a wax model which belonged in Madame Tussauds, than ever, caught his eye and jerked her head in the direction of the back room.

Frowning; and thinking what the hell now? Dev reluctantly followed her through.

Before he was fully in the room, Mrs Archer grabbed his collar and quickly yanked him through the door, slamming it shut behind him with her foot.

'Tell me you have nothing to do with that dead shopkeeper. Talk you bastard... And it better be what I want to hear.'

'What fucking shopkeeper? You stupid barmy git.'

She glared at him, as her hand tightened on his collar, twisting it until she nearly had him in a strangle hold.

'What you on about?' Dev snapped, jerking himself free of her grip, and quickly stepping away from her.

'Him off the Seahills shop...Mr, err...Jansen, that's him...Found murdered this morning.'

'No way!'

'Way.'

For a moment Dev stared at her, his mind working overtime and he started to panic and shook his head. 'No...The old bastard was alright when I left, I know he was.' He muttered out loud without realising it.

'What?' Mrs Archer practically screamed in his face.

Dev stared at her for a moment before muttering. 'I was in earlier, for some milk okay, and when I left the fucking dickhead was alright I swear.'

'You swear,' she laughed. 'That's gotta be the joke of the fucking century.'

'Yes I swear...Look it's got nothing to do with me what ever happened to the old fart.'

'Why don't I believe you?'

'Fuck you.'

She reached for his throat but he quickly stepped away. 'I've told you it's nothing to do with me.'

'So you didn't upset him in any way?'

'I swear.'

'Again... Well fucking well pardon me if I find that so hard to believe-again.'

Dev clenched his fists, and with one swipe of his arm he sent everything on the desk in front of him crashing to the floor. 'It fucking wasn't me,' he yelled. 'How many bastard times do I have to say, for fucks sake?'

Mrs Archer's eyes narrowed as she looked him up and down. 'Anyone see you in the shop?'

He shook his head. 'No, it was empty.'

'Outside?'

He shrugged. 'Don't think so. The whole place was deserted. Sunday morning, probs all sleeping last night's booze off. Except for a couple of fools having a full scale battle in the street, and he didn't see me.'

'What about the other one?'

'Guess she was in a bad enough state not to remember. To busy feeling sorry for herself, cos the love of her life had fucking dumped her.'

He made no mention of the fact that he had helped the woman. To show any kind of weakness in front of Mrs Archer, or anyone- was not a good thing.

'You hope.' She went on.

Dev shrugged. 'Who's bothered...And I've told you it wasn't me...That should be enough.'

'Not good enough,' she shouted, angered by his seeming complacency. 'We need to know if anyone saw you in or around the friggin' shop.'

'For fuck's sake why?'

She sighed. 'Because obviously dim wit, I want nothing to lead the coppers here. Cos trust me if they come sniffing you will suffer, big time.'

He shook his head in frustration as he gritted his teeth and spat the words out. 'I saw nobody, the street was fucking deserted apart from those two, and they were too fucking busy to care about anything or anybody. For fucks sake, ten thousand could have been there and they wouldn't have given a damn...It wasn't me...How many times?'

'Right then, so apparently you've got nowt to worry about then, have you?'

For a brief moment he stared silently at her. Then slowly shook his head.

'Hmm.' She walked back and forwards in front of him keeping eye contact, he didn't once flinch, though the threat she posed was visible in every step she took.

After a minute she stopped in front of him, her face only inches from his. 'That's if you are truly innocent, which I find damn hard to believe,' she smirked at him. 'Pick this fucking mess up now, and pray that nothings broken because believe me, then you will have something to worry about, punk.'

He watched her go, his eyes boring into her back, then slowly unclenching his fists, he walked over to the window. Moving the curtain to one side, he gasped as a familiar figure walked past. For the moment all thoughts of the dead shopkeeper left him as a sly smile played on his lips. He watched her walk by, his mind once again obsessed with revenge.

'You'll pay,' he muttered. 'You will all pay, every fucking one of you...And soon, very soon.' His hands clasped tightly at his side as she disappeared from view. He leaned further into the window to catch a last glance of her, then she was gone, leaning back against the wall he took a deep breath.

In the bar Mrs Archer was talking to a man in the corner. He watched as she poured him a small glass of whiskey.

'You sure he can be trusted?' The man who was short stocky dark haired, with a thick beard, and a heavy east European accent, asked as he picked the glass up.

'As much as any of the toe-rags around here can, bit of a rare breed, deals them but doesn't do them.'

'Right then if you say so; I've just found out that the new shipment arrives tonight, something I didn't know on your visit this morning, the van should be here around three am, all being well.'

Mrs Archer smiled, a soulless smile that stretched her heavily botoxed lips, but never reached her eyes.

Half an hour later she was back in the back room, her eyes flicked to the desk noting that everything had been picked up and put back in place. She looked at Dev. For a moment there was silence, then glowering at her Dev said. 'What?'

'I have another job for you.'

'Okay.' He looked suspiciously at her.

'But first, do you have a passport?'

'No- Why?'

'Just that the new work requires a passport.'

'What sort of work?'

'You'll find out in good time.'

'As in flying?'

'Perhaps.'

'When?'

'Possibly tomorrow.'

'No way.'

'Err...Yes! An opportunity to see the world and be paid for it, bet you never once dreamed of that in your dirty stinking prison cell did you?'

Dev stared at her. No, he thought. No way.

Her eyes narrowed as she said 'You're not frightened of flying are you?'

Shaking his head, Dev backed away. 'No.'

He had other things to do, things that were important to him. Things that needed sorting, and being a permanent skivvy for this ugly freak wasn't one of them.

'No.' He repeated.

'You what?' Unused to being refused anything, Mrs Archer stared at him for a moment. 'You will do what I say. When I say, and remember by your own admission, you were the last one to see the shopkeeper alive,' she smiled at him. 'And remember, you owe me big time, the missing woman from the Seahills, remember her?' One word in the right ear, that's all. '

'You wouldn't?' For a moment Dev felt the prickles of fear run through him, and actually felt physically sick. Then he reasoned with himself that this woman would be the last person on earth who would get involved with the police. No she was definitely bluffing, she had to be.

She raised one eyebrow as she stared silently at him.

'Can't anyhow, just got out of prison,' he shrugged and said sarcastically. 'Don't think you can get a passport right off. You have to be a good boy to get one of them!'

She laughed. 'Fool, do you think that's a problem? Tonight when you come to pick up the latest goods, there will be a friend of mine waiting, he'll take your pass port picture the rest is easily sorted. Trust me.'

'No,' he'd come this far, nothing was going to stop him now. He had plans and the ugly bitch can shove her job up her arse. 'No.' He repeated, backing towards the door.

'No,' she stared at him. 'How dare you?' She stood up. 'How fucking dare you?' She demanded.

By now he was at the door and yanking it open. Turning to her, he said. 'There are things I have to do, and trust me...Your dirty work isn't one of them, at least for the next week.'

'What..?'

'I'll be back for the job tonight. Then I'm missing for a few days,' he shrugged. 'A few days or forever.'

'And what could be so important in your pathetic life?'

'I have a party to go to.'

## CHAPTER FORTY

The interview with Alfie Grossmont had gone smoothly; the man had been compliant all of the time answering questions politely, and insisting over and over, with a polite smile, that he was innocent. And that he also had more than one witness to prove where he was.

Behind her desk, Lorraine sat with her elbows resting on the desk top, and her chin resting on her hands, she was starring at the wall in front of her, where pictures of the dead man and Alfie Grossmont, were pinned.

'Well he certainly, without any doubt has the strength to tear the scalp off, Jesus just look at the friggin size of him. But; it doesn't fit with the actual murder's he's already admitted to- and served time for. And, I have a feeling,' she shook her head. 'Something's not right.' She stood up and moved over to the wall, again staring at Grossmont's photograph.

'Yes I know,' Sanderson said. 'The other scalps were all cut off not ripped, like...Like.' He gestured with his hand towards the pictures on the wall. 'That has got to be one very angry man to do something like that. Who knows, all that time in jail he could have been dwelling on it. A lot of years, a lot of anger, it can do really bad things to a person.'

'Probably didn't have the strength back then- that he has now though,' Dinwall finally finished with his parking fines, put in. 'Remember he was just a young'un back then.'

Sanderson shrugged. 'The alternative is not good.'

'No it isn't, but to be honest and my gut feeling, I really don't think it's him.' Lorraine shook her head as she glanced at her watch, and was about to say, it's time Luke was back, when he walked in.

'Okay Luke, what have you got for us?' Lorraine looked up at him.

'Rock solid alibi, just like Morpeh said. He was out most of that night with a cat rescue group in Consett...Consett cats, rescuing feral kittens. Three very reliable witnesses are adamant he was with them all insisting that animals of all kinds, just love him to bits.'

Lorraine sighed. 'Guess that's it then. Dinwall, take him back to Morpeth.'

'I'll do it,' Sanderson rose out of his chair. 'Need to stretch the legs a bit.'

'Fine by me boss,' Dinwall shrugged. 'As long as I don't have to go with him.'

'Take a PC with you Sanderson.'

'Sure thing boss.'

'Well then, it looks like we have a particular vicious murderer on the loose, and we can't keep it under wraps any longer, it wasn' exactly fucking private was it. I mean.' she held her hands ou palms up. 'The Glass centre roof, for God's sake. God only knows what rumours are flying around.'

'Yup boss, the press were already gathering at the door when came in, demanding to know what was going on, not only abou the Glass centre, but about the Seahills shopkeeper as well. The whole of the Seahills estate is running scared.' Luke sat back in his chair. 'In fact from what I hear most of the lousy low life's are running scared, never mind the ordinary good people.'

'Shit.' Lorraine pulled the other folder towards her and flickec it open. 'That's all we need people running scared, and by the time the papers get a hold of it.' She looked up at the ceiling and shook her head in dismay.

'Who was on duty?' Luke asked.

'DI Stella Hawkes from Chester Le Street,' Lorraine frowned 'Actually, I've never met the woman.' She glanced from Dinwal to Luke, 'Anybody?'

Dinwall looked from his computer as Sanderson left withou

replying. 'Well I met her last year, when I had to go to court on that case when the wife turned out to be telling nothing but a whole bunch of bloody lies, about her husband, and her poor parents which she used to beat up on a regular basis, as well as her neighbours...Remember, it was in all the papers...Right bloody nutter she was. And still the daft judge took pity on her, six months suspended sentence...Should have been locked up for six years, the trouble she caused.'

'I'm asking about Detective Inspector Hawkes, not the bloody nutter's life story.'

'Just saying.'

'Well!'

'Oh, yes Hawkes- guess she's alright.'

'And that's it?'

'Well, she's got black hair, about your size. She's been based in Chester Le Street for about a year or so, originally from somewhere in South London.'

'That's a pretty big area.' Luke said.

'Kingston, I think...Well it might be...or, yes it's definitely the Kingston area.'

Luke glanced at Lorraine with a wry smile. 'He seems to know a lot about a woman he only met once?'

'Doesn't he just.'

'It's me job.' Dinwall grinned.

They all looked at the door a moment later when there was a single knock, followed by two others.

'Come in.' Lorraine said.

The door opened and a dark haired woman walked in. She approached Lorraine's desk, held out her hand and said with a smile, 'Hi, I'm DI Stella Hawkes.'

'Lorraine Hunt.' Lorraine shook her hand, thinking, talk about the devil!

At first glance she thought the woman seemed pleasant enough, a bit on the plump side, and the small scar running to her hairline from the corner of her right eye didn't do her any favours, but her navy blue suit was smart, although she herself would never have matched it with a red blouse for work, but the woman's smile seemed genuine and certainly reached her dark eyes. Her hair was in a neat plait which was wrapped around her head and kept in place with pins which matched her blouse.

Before Lorraine could ask her why she was here, Dinwall was at the woman's side. 'Hello, remember me?' His smile was wide and practically cracking his face in half.

DI Hawkes looked him up and down. Shaking her head she said. 'No sorry...Have we met before?'

Suppressing a grin, Lorraine glanced over at Luke.

'Well only...Just briefly like...Last year...In court. Remember that crazy woman?'

'Which one would that be?'

'You know the one who...'

Before Dinwall could dig himself deeper into a corner, Luke carried a chair over and put it in front of Lorraine's desk. 'Hi I'm DS Luke Daniels. Please, take a seat.'

'Thank you.' She smiled, her eyes lingering longer than they needed to- Lorraine was thinking- over Luke.

'I thought a courtesy call was in order, also to pick your brains to see if there was any reason that you could know of, why someone should want to murder Mr Jansen.'

'So it is murder?' Lorraine frowned. 'We were wondering what had gone on.'

'Well, the man has a staple gun embedded in his forehead, also a fractured nose, which could have been caused by an upper punch as opposed to a straight on punch, although the autopsy isn't due until later tonight.'

'So you're after picking our brains for a motive?'

'Well something like that, seeing as you all know the area, and the inhabitants.'

'All I can say is that he was a pretty nice guy. Great with the local kids. Most of which had a lot of time for him... He and his wife have lived here all of their life, no children of their own. And no enemy's that I know of. You heard otherwise?' She looked from Luke, to Dinwall.'

'No.' Luke replied, while Dinwall shook his head.

'A robbery?' Lorraine asked.

DI Hawkes shrugged. 'There was money in the till, so I doubt it, too early for much cash probably just his start of the day change...I'm organising a house to house, see if anyone remembers someone being in the area at the time,' she rose from her chair. 'Any how I won't keep you any longer...Thanks for your time.'

'No problem, if we hear anything we will be in touch immediately. Although I honestly think if anyone saw anything going on in the shop, he was so well respected it would most definitely have been reported. Is there anything else I can help you with?'

Hawkes sat back down. 'Well there is one other thing, which really shouldn't be a problem, it concerns the family we have in the safe house on one of your estates.'

'Oh yes. I took the call from DS Steel. One of mine, PC Carter, got her and her kids safely in early this morning...There's not a problem is there?'

'No, not really it was just a slight worry with there being what may be a murder on the same day that they move in, I mean what are the odds on that?'

'I can understand your concern.'

'Anyhow, thanks for your cooperation.'

'No bother, if you need us, we're here.'

When she'd gone Lorraine shrugged. 'She seems nice enough, hope the hell she catches the low life.'

'You mean the lousy swine who did that to Mr Jenson...You wish it had been our case, don't you?' Luke asked.

'Well, technically...' Lorraine mulled it over. 'It really should be ours.'

'Technically we don't have the time to sort two totally unrelated murders. Especially with half of Sunderland down with the damn bug.'

'You're right.' Standing she went to the small fridge on the bench by the window and took out a can of diet coke.

'Can I have one of those boss?' Dinwall asked. 'Please, dying of thirst here.'

Lorraine took another can out, and with a frown banged it down on Dinwall's desk.

Dinwall looked wide eyed at Luke and made a perfect circle with his mouth as he opened the tab. 'Anyhow,' he said after taking a huge gulp. 'I was wondering if the cases might possibly be related in some way.'

'What?' Lorraine asked.

'The two cases, you know the shopkeeper and the people in the safe house. Hawkes might be right.'

'Now that I very much doubt...Where's your reasoning in that idea?'

Dinwall shrugged. 'Just bouncing a few ideas around.'

A moment later the phone on Lorraine's desk started ringing. Snatching it up and putting it to her ear, she said 'Detective Inspector Lorraine Hunt.'

Listening to the voice on the other end, her eyebrows raised as she looked at Luke. She put the phone down a few minutes later and with a sigh she looked from Luke to Dinwall. 'There's been another body found.'

'Shit.' Luke said. 'Where?'

'Scalped?' Dinwall asked.

'Yes...This one's further along the coast, nearly at South Shields, around the Marsden area, beside the Marsden Grotto, to be exact.'

'And.'

'This one is the body of a young woman she's been dead for a while though.'

'So we do have a serial killer on our hands.'

'Yes. Exactly what we didn't want'

'God only knows how many others there are out there then. Could be a dozen or more.' Dinwall shook his head.

'Look on the black side why don't you.' Luke said.

'Okay, Dinwall, get Carter in here to man the fort, while youse two come with me.'

Half an hour later they were staring down at the body of a young woman. Scottie was standing by the woman's head. Lorraine moved to the right side, while Dinwall and Luke hovered together on the left.

'She's around the thirty three age group. As you can see it's exactly the same type of scalping as the man on the glass centre roof. Her scalp has also been half cut and half torn off. Plus, she's been in the water for about two to three months; she's covered in the early stages of grave wax. And I'm afraid a lot of what damage you see is down to the fish and crabs, they go for the soft parts on the face, the lips and the eyes.'

'What the hell is grave wax?' Luke asked.

'Well, roughly speaking a body lasts longer where no flies can get to it, like in the sea. Grave wax is basically body fat, it's a crumbly white waxy substance which grows on the parts of the body that contain fat, cheeks, stomach, bottom, breasts.'

Luke, starting to feel queasy was seriously regretting asking

Scottie the question in the first place.'

'Basically it's a chemical reaction...'

'Enough.' Luke held his hand up.

'Well you did ask.'

'Alright, we get the picture...Whoever this crazy bastard is; he's a power freak alright. How the hell...' Lorraine looked at the woman's face, knowing that she herself could have been lying on the same slab not so long ago. Suddenly she felt sick. Taking a deep breath, she pulled herself together.

Still looking at the body, Scottie nodded. 'He is that alright Lorraine, and as strong as an ox...Also, as with the previous body, this one bears many scars. Old and new,' he lifted her right arm up. 'Look here.' A seven inch ragged scar ran down her side from her armpit to her waist.

'Poor bugger that looks like it's been well and truly left to heal itself.' Dinwall said.

'It has. It also happened some time in her teens. Also there is evidence of many broken bones. Her right arm is the most recent break and it was left to heal itself...And she must have been thrown in the water almost immediately after she was scalped, perhaps she might even have been still alive.'

'Oh my God.' Lorraine said quietly.

'Hmm, wonder if they knew each other?' Dinwall asked.

'I'm thinking the same.' Luke added. 'Is she the same nationality as the first guy?'

'No, she's English.'

'Has a search been made of the area?' Luke asked.

'As far as I know it's ongoing. One thing they both had in common though, is sand.'

'Sand?' Lorraine frowned.

'Well you know what they say, sand gets everywhere. We found small traces in both their pockets. Also in the girls left big toe nail. And one of her finger nails. And the man's right hand had traces of sand all over it.'

'Which means they both lived very close to the beach, or both recently visited the beach?' Luke said.

'One or the other, I'm thinking they lived very close, but you're right they could have been visiting. Plus the girl was going to have sand on her anyhow.'

'Dinwall, get onto the dog warden for the area, see if any strays have been found wandering around.'

'Why?'

'Because.' Luke looked at him. 'If any stray dogs have been picked up in the area in the last few months, then chances are they'll be chipped, and lead us straight to the owners address, which could be one or both of the victims, who might have been walking their dogs when attacked.'

'Oh, right.'

'One other thing.'

Lorraine swung her head towards Scottie, wondering what else he'd come up with.

'She had recently to her death, given birth.'

'Oh dear, well we can check the hospital records, that might be a help in finding out who she is. Anyhow time to go, phone me with the rest of the results Scottie, please.' Without waiting for his answer Lorraine turned on her heel and walked out.

Scottie frowned at Luke, who shrugged then followed Dinwall out of the door.

## CHAPTER FORTY ONE

After tea was over, and unaware that she was being watched Suzy made her way back to the swings. She'd been told over and over by just about everybody in the whole family, to keep out of Robbie's way in case she spilled the beans about his birthday party.

'Hmm,' she huffed, too herself. 'Like I can't keep a secret, course I can...Kept loads of secrets.'

Rounding the corner she saw that not only the swings, but the whole playing field was empty. Where's Molly? She wondered, looking around.

At first she hadn't liked Molly, thought she was nowt but a snob, that's what Emma had called her, when she'd told her about her new friend, because now they were friends. And she had kept Molly's secret, she had only told Emma, and sisters didn't count where secrets were, most times.

'Well that's what our Emma says anyhow.' Suzy said to herself, as she bent down and plucked a couple of early budding buttercups out of the grass. 'And I never told the coppers when they knocked on the door either.'

Just then Molly arrived back in the park; she jumped on the nearest swing, as unaware as Suzy was that she was being watched.

'I can go higher than you.' She yelled, standing on the swing.

'Can not.' Suzy laughed, jumping on the next swing.

Higher and higher they went, bending their knees and thrusting their body's as hard as they could, competing to see who would get level with the top bar first. The wind ruffled their hair as they giggled.

Silently the watcher dropped the curtain, wondering who the new girl was, but frightened to go and find out in case Dev was out there, waiting for her.

## CHAPTER FORTY TWO

He took a deep breath; the air still seemed fresh, even though he was certain more than five hours had gone by. He felt anger rising up in him with panic close behind. And forced himself to again breathe deeply and slowly.

Just because the air still seemed fresh, doesn't mean that I have to waste it.

Never the sort of person to feel sorry for himself, in this situation he guessed that anyone would. He wished to God, for how many times he couldn't remember, that night had never happened. But it had, and he and his brother tried to help as any decent person would.

Would they though?

In this day and age, wasn't it safer to turn and walk away?

Why hadn't they?

Damn!

Again he brought himself under control, but why?

What's the point in saving air?

I'm only going to drag it out.

He thought of banging his head, over and over until he knocked himself out, or hopefully killed himself. But he could barely reach the lid of the coffin with his hands.

He wondered briefly why he couldn't feel the sides of the coffin, just empty space.

Please God help me.

For a moment his thoughts turned to his brother, wondering where he was, if he was even still alive.

A sudden huge shiver brought him back to his own plight. He nearly laughed out loud at the thought of catching pneumonia, as if it mattered, he would be long dead before that set in.

He shivered again, wasn't there an old saying. 'As cold as the grave.'

## CHAPTER FORTY THREE

The woman's screams echoed around the dirty cream painted walls, there were no windows in the dark cell like room. The floor was made up of stone slabs with old dried marks of blood in the many cracks- which no amount of scrubbing over the past years could erase. There was one locked door in the room.

She lay flat on her back with her knees forced open by another's hands, and her legs pushed up close to her chest. She grabbed the sides of the bed with her hands, gripping tightly and praying hard, praying to any God who would listen to release her from her torment, a torment that had gone on for hours, and was getting worse by the minute.

'No.' she screamed. 'I can't take any more.'

'Stop.'

'Please, please make it stop.' She sobbed. She let go of the bed with her right hand and began pounding on the man's arm, as hard as she could, over and over.

'I can't do this.' She sobbed.

Both of her hands were grabbed and held tightly, as a man's

voice above her, quietly said. 'Yes you can, you will- because you have no choice.'

'No.' she thrashed from side to side.

Standing behind her he moved his grip further up her arms, digging his nails into her soft flesh, squeezing. 'You will do this, and shut the fuck up while you're doing it.'

'No...I can't do it.'

'You have no choice.'

'No...No...It hurts.' She screamed even louder.

'Shut up bitch.' He growled at her.

'Push. Now.' A woman beside her said.

'I fucking am.' She yelled back at her.

'Again.'

'Can't...Can't do it no more,' she sobbed. 'Please make it stop. Just make it go away.' Pulling her right arm free she punched the bed over and over.

Behind her the man grabbed her arm back, twisting it savagely as he growled. 'You'll do as you're told bitch. If you know what's good for you.'

She started to cry, thinking of her mother and her father, her brothers, her sister -and wanting them all more than she ever had at this moment, and wishing more than ever that she had not got drunk that night and went off with a perfect stranger, just to piss her boyfriend off. How many times as a kid had she been told never to go off with strangers, uncountable, then as a teenager who knows it all, every warning is totally forgotten. And now she was paying for all she had put them through. Ten months since that fateful night. Ten months of hell.

'Fool.' She muttered.

'Why, why?'

As if reading her mind the man above her laughed, as the pain even worse than before coursed through her body.

Weary and drained, with a picture of her whole family staring out of the window looking for her, entered her mind, she barely muttered. 'No.'

'Yes you can...You have to. Come on, one more push. You have to do this, you know what will happen if you give up. Come on, try harder.'

'No, no, no, this time she managed a weak scream. At that moment she couldn't care less what would happen, she felt as if her whole insides were being ripped out.

'That's it... Good-Good...It's coming.'

'What? Oh my God.'

'One more push.'

'You keep saying.'

'Come on, come on. You can't give up now.'

The woman, young, her blonde hair tied up at the back, her huge green eyes bulging, had been in labour for ten hours, with no pain relief at all. During that time she and the woman acting as a midwife had been alone. Until a knock on the door, had brought the man named Draco in

From somewhere she found the strength for one more loud scream, which reached a glass shattering pitch, then slowly ebbed. For a moment there was silence. Both the man and the new mother stared at the woman.

'Please,' the new mother begged. Her heart sank as she thought the worst. 'Is...Is...'

The man and the midwife looked from the baby to the mother. Then the cry of a newborn invaded the room. He grinned at her.

'Oh my God...Oh my God. What is it?

'Is it alright?'

'Give it to me.'

'Best you don't know.' Quickly the woman cut the cord, wrapped the baby up in a grubby grey towel and handed it over to the man.

He gave it the once over, then turned to go.

'My baby.' The new mother screamed.

At the door, the man turned back and shook his head. 'Shh you knew it would be so bitch,' he grinned. 'Might let you keep the next one, or the one after that.'

A moment later the door slammed behind him, leaving an echo the woman would never forget.

'No...No...No...Please,' she begged.' Please, please, bring my baby back.'

The door closed silently behind the man's back.

The mother tried to get out of bed, but was stopped by the woman. 'No, you've had a hard time; you need to rest- You know they won't send for a doctor.' She shook her head.

'Please, please,' the mother begged again. 'Tell me what it is.'

'You know that's more than my life's worth.'

## CHAPTER FORTY FOUR

When Mr Skillings arrived back triumphant at the Seahills with Doris and Dolly in tow, both scowling behind his back, it was to find the place filled with even more rumours of Mr Jenson's murder. As he was holding out his arm to help Doris off the bus, Jacko stepped forward.

'I've got her, Mr Skillings.'

Before Mr Skillings could answer, seventy two year old Josie Bunting, wearing the latest sports gear and trainers in trendy pale blues, from Daffodil close, and who was walking past looked at him and said. 'Bloody awful about the shopkeeper isn't it? Beating him up and then stabbing him, no need for it-lovely man he was. They want to do the same to them, that's what I say.'

'Aye.' Doris chimed in as clinging onto Jacko's arm she stepped off the bus. 'Talk of the bowling club it was.' She stopped herself from saying what she was really thinking, you weren't feeling sorry for him when you were nicking his cheese biscuits and bars of soap, you greedy old bitch, instead she went on. 'Time them bloody coppers got their act together, people are not safe in their beds these days.'

Behind her Dolly declined Mr Skillings arm, and stepped down herself. 'That's true enough.' She nodded her head.

'Well, it's all over the place that he was murdered, but nowt been said officially like.' Jacko said.

'That's cos they don't bloody well want you to know what's going on,' Dolly pulled her coat tightly around her. 'I'll catch you later.' She headed off in the direction of home, still in the huff because Mr Skillings had fairly beaten them today.

Mr Skillings shrugged, as Jacko said with a smile. 'You been upsetting the ladies Mr Skillings?'

'Not me lad.' Mr Skillings grinned. 'Why would they be upset over a game of bloody bowls?'

'Doesn't matter who won...Not the end of the world, is it?' Doris tossed her head, with a huge sniff of her nose.

'Oh dear.' Jacko muttered, smiling wryly at Mr Skillings.

Mr Skillings gave Jacko a return smile, before saying, 'What's what's going on here like?' As he watched three squad cars come down the street, behind Jacko.

'Oh, another murder do you think?' Dolly Smith who hadn't taken barely a step away asked, her eyes wide.

'Bloody hell I hope not.' Doris said.

'Betcha it is.' Dolly nodded with conviction.

'It's the coppers knocking on doors.' Josie said as she walked away.

'Err, one murder is enough for today, don't you think?' Mr Skillings shook his head.

'I don't get it,' Jacko said. 'Who the hell would want to kill a good bloke like him?'

'God only knows what the hell goes on in people's heads these days...Shocking.' Mr Skillings stared after the passing police car.

'I know.' Dolly agreed.

'Robbery I heard, up at the club, stabbed him right through the heart. Swines.' Mr Skillings said, straining his neck to keep the cars in sight.

## CHAPTER FORTY FIVE

'What the hell are you talking about our Emma?' Kerry looked away from her phone.

'Them one's over there, the new people,' she pointed out of the window. 'Them, they're on the run.'

'More daft rubbish.' Kerry looked back at her phone. Another string of smiley faces.

'For fuck's sake.' She threw her phone onto the settee, where it bounced and landed on the floor.

'I'm gonna tell mam.'

'What..? No not you...I didn't mean you honestly our Emma.'

Emma was glaring at Kerry, her bottom lip quivering, 'I'm still gonna tell mam.'

'No, just tell me, I promise I'll listen.'

'You never listen to me.'

'Promise I will.'

'Our Suzy's new friend, them what's moved in over the road. She say's they're on the run.'

'From what?' Kerry tried not to smile.

Emma shrugged. 'I don't know do I?'

'Take no notice Emma our Suzy will be day dreaming again. You know what she's like, the kid just makes it up as she goes along.' Kerry picked her phone up. 'Anyhow I've got bigger things to worry about.'

'Knew it. You always have.' Emma stormed out of the sitting room, and reached the kitchen just as Sandra came in through the back door.

'What's the matter with you?'

'Nowt.' Emma replied.

'Yes there is, you've got a face like thunder.'

'It's our Kerry she never listens to me.'

'Never mind, sometimes big sisters are like that Emma. So where's your mam?'

'She took Mr Skillings washing over, cos his washer's broke... Again.'

'Oh yes, so it is,' she frowned. 'But I thought he got it the daft thing mended.'

'He did, but it broke again. That's three times it broke, I think he just likes mam to do his washing.'

'Oh dear. 'Sandra hid a smile. 'Anyhow, you can tell me if something's bothering you pet. Come on, I'm all ears.'

'It's not bothering me, really. It's just our Suzy says them new people over the road are on the run, cos she's friends with the girl the one who lives there now. I was just telling our Kerry that's all, but she's always got something better to do than listen to me.'

'Well I'm listening...Who are they on the run from?' Sandra bit her bottom lip. Suzy was well known for her tall stories, and she was surprised that Emma had fallen for this one.

Neither of them heard Vicky Drysdon from number ten Daffodil close come up the back steps, to borrow a cup of sugar as Emma began talking.

About to knock on the door, she paused as Emma's shrill voice told Sandra, everything that Molly had told Suzy. Deciding to borrow the sugar elsewhere, Vicky hurried to Mrs Bowmont's house further down the road and proceeded to tell her about the new neighbours. Later her husband passed the information onto his friend's in the Blue Lion, unaware that Mrs Archer was listening to everything that was said.

## CHAPTER FORTY SIX

Lorraine and Luke arrived at her mother's house at six thirty; the door was opened as they were halfway up the path by her mother's best friend Peggy. Peggy being her usual self welcomed them with open arms only somehow she didn't have quite enough arm length to encompass Lorraine as well.

'Well hello Luke you lovely, lovely man,' she beamed at him. Throwing Lorraine a 'Hi kid,' and a smile as she passed, then looking quickly back at Luke. 'I have made one of my specials just for you love.'

Shaking her head while hiding a smile, because she was used to playing second fiddle to any member of the male species where Peggy was, Lorraine went into her mother's sitting room.

Mavis a relic of the hippy years, her blonde hair tied up with a flowing chiffon pink and yellow scarf, wore a long pink dress with bunches of many coloured wild flowers scattered all over it.

'Hello mam. And what are you doing out of bed? Thought the doc said you needed total rest.'

'Feeling much better pet.'

Lorraine held her mother at arm's length as she looked her over. 'Please,' she whispered. 'Promise me you won't go out in that get up.'

'Why ever not pet? 'Mavis grinned.

'Because you look like someone just scattered a packet of seeds over you.'

Mavis tutted and spun round in a full circle. 'Like you haven't said that before, and I'm sure Luke doesn't think so, do you love?'

'Of course not Mavis, you would look good in anything.' Luke replied with a grin, as Peggy shamelessly put herself between them and smiled coyly at Luke.

'You too Peggy.'

'Well thank you kind sir.' Peggy curtsied, as Mavis pushed her out of the way and kissed Luke's cheek.

'Hmm, is that the aftershave I bought you for Christmas pet?'

'It certainly is.' Luke replied, then thought. Shit, Peggy bought the same aftershave. He looked quickly round, but she must have gone into the kitchen. Thank God for that, he thought.

Turning to Lorraine Mavis said. 'This one's a keeper pet, much better than...What's his name?'

'Mother!'

An hour later, having eaten a roast beef dinner made by Mavis, and helped by Peggy, which she frequently reminded them of, and who now sat opposite Luke and Lorraine in the sitting room, while Peggy washed the dishes, Mavis, ignoring a warning look from Luke, who had caught her earlier in the kitchen and had told her of his worry for Lorraine, said. 'Okay pet, so when are you going to put this lousy business behind you and move on?'

Lorraine spun round and glared at Luke.

'Don't look at him love, I can see for myself what it's done to you...I am after all your mother and believe it or not, I know when there's something wrong...Is there no where that you can get help, I thought the police had those sort of doctors.'

'Those sort of doctors!' Lorraine frowned at her mother, while Luke stared at the fireplace.

'You know what I mean.'

Lorraine sighed. The last thing she wanted was her mother on the case.

Mavis stood and walked over to Lorraine, patting her arm, she said. 'We all need a little help now and then pet, and it's still a couple of days till the court case.'

'Mother I'm fine okay, so there's nowt for you to be worrying about. Duke, come on walkies.'

Mavis shook her head.

Excited Duke jumped up from in front of the fire, and tail

wagging he made his way into the kitchen where his leader was kept. Silently Lorraine followed him.

As soon as Mavis heard the back door close she turned to Luke. 'Go on follow her.'

Luke shook his head. 'Mavis, she won't let me in, I've tried over and over.'

'Yes well obviously not enough. Go after her...Go on. And it's time to do what I said.'

Luke hesitated a moment, before meeting Mavis's eyes, then he muttered. 'Okay, you're right.'

Outside Luke wondered which way she had gone. Deciding she probably went left towards the park he headed that way. Again he wondered what to say to her, really he had said more than once everything he could think of and he was seriously beginning to wonder if the court case would really be an end of it. He mulled it over again as he kept on walking.

Only, Lorraine, instead of going towards the park, had headed towards the beck, the opposite direction to the one Luke thought she had taken.

Full dark had fallen as she neared the bridge over the beck. She let Duke off for a run in the surrounding fields and looped his leader around her hand. The beck, a small stream running behind the Burnside estate had been there for as long as anyone could remember. A copse of trees to her right made the night seem even darker. She decided she would turn when she reached the bridge, even though she knew the ground extremely well; the very last thing she wanted to do was trip and break a bone or two. She frowned, suddenly realising just how quiet it was, pausing in midstride she peered into the dark.

'Where the hell's Duke,' she muttered. 'Duke.' She shouted a moment later, breaking the silence.

She frowned again as her voice echoed but there was no sight or sound of the dog, her heart beat rose as she slowly looked around her. Is that footsteps?' she thought. She strained her ears but it had fallen silent again.

'Duke,' she yelled. 'Duke.'

Where the hell?

A moment later she heard rustling in the grass beside her quickly she stepped backwards. Anything could be in there. She shuddered. Snakes even, just because no one ever saw them doesn't mean they aren't there.

'Shit!'

If there was one thing Lorraine hated in the world it was most definitely snakes. For as long as she could remember she'd had a thing about them. Spiders, beetles, didn't bother her, rats even, but snakes, no way.

Suddenly the grass parted and Duke came bounding out, nearly knocking her over in his frenzy to greet her.

She heaved a sigh of relief, then froze again as the grass rustled once more.

'Shit. What the hell.' A second later Luke stepped out.

He had realised soon enough that he had gone the wrong way and quickly doubled back.

'Friggin hell Luke,' Lorraine rested her hand on her chest. 'You trying to give me a heart attack or what?'

'Sorry, Duke had got himself trapped in somebody's back garden way back there, the gate must have been open and he wondered in and it must have swung shut behind him.'

'Daft dog,' Lorraine ruffled the top of Duke's head. 'I thought it was a flaming snake.'

After a few moments awkward silence, Luke stepped forward and put his right arm over Lorraine's shoulder. He felt her stiffen under his touch and his heart sank.

'Lorraine,' he murmured. 'Please don't do this.'

'Do what?' she pulled away from him.

'You know what...It's gone on long enough. Just talk to me.' He practically begged as she stared at him.

But she turned away and said. 'Come on, time we were getting back,' clipping Duke's lead on she started walking away. 'Come on Duke.' She practically shouted.

'No Lorraine you walk away now and it's over. I mean it Lorraine.'

'What?' She spun round.

'You heard me, it can't go on. I can't go on creeping around on eggshells never knowing what might set you off. From one day to the next.' As he said the words, his heart sank, but he knew it couldn't go on any longer. Something had to be done to shake her up, to get her back, and this was a risk he had to take.

Lorraine's shoulders slumped as looking at him she sadly shook her head.

'I love you Luke.' She whispered.

'Then let me in.'

## CHAPTER FORTY SEVEN

Dragging his feet slowly from the car which he'd had to park right at the bottom of the street yet again, Carter opened his front door, wondering how the hell he could avoid his mother for the next month or so, or even the next year, and fully regretting telling her that he had something to tell her.

God, she's like a ferret, she won't forget. Damn! I know she won't. With a sigh like a condemned man, he hung his coat up on the rail behind the door.

'Is that you?' he heard her say a moment later, he practically cringed as he walked into the sitting room.

'Expecting somebody else were you? I mean you get so many visitors don't you mam?'

'Don't be flippant with me.' She pulled her lilac blouse down, before patting her hair.

'Sorry.' He mumbled, sitting in the opposite chair. His mother had a love of anything and everything green, sometimes Carter felt as if he was living in the middle of a field, he swore if one more potted plant made its way into the sitting room he would throw it out of the window.

Not that he ever would, his mother was too much of a force to be reckoned with, but he would love to. He pictured picking the huge fat leaved plant with the foreign sounding name up off the table and throwing it, right at the huge mirror above the fire place then seeing her face, he immediately felt guilty. His mother was a good woman and a good mother. It had just been the two of them since his father had walked out when he was five.

He could barely remember his face, and his mother had long ago burned all photographs of him, he wondered if he reminded her of him, because the only thing he'd ever had in common with his mother had been the colour of their hair.

Shit he would have to tell her.

And now.

Go for it.

But just as he was drumming up the courage, to tell her what he'd wanted to for a long while now, she said. 'So is this right about a murder down the Seahills shop this morning, nowt on the news, or in the Sunderland echo about it though. Only Mr Sandley next door is totally adamant about it. Swears everybody in Houghton is talking about it, vicious it was an' 0all, poor man had his throat cut. And apparently, who ever done it had tried to start a fire, destroy the evidence like. Only there's nowt in here about it,' she waved her Sunderland Echo at him. 'I mean you would think that it would be in the flaming local rag wouldn't you?'

'Not much I can say mam; you know that, its police business we've been through this before.'

'Aye that'll be right, I'm the only person in the street with a copper in the family, and I'm always the last to know if anything goes on...' She tutted as she frowned at him.

Carter shrugged. 'What's for tea?'

'Fancy a Chinese take away son? Can't be bothered to cook anything now, had a migraine most of the bloody day,' she rubbed her temples. 'I hope it doesn't get any worse, might be that I need something to eat, but these flashing lights in me eyes son, bloody awful, they are.'

'Err...What?' This was not the question he'd been expecting and for a moment it threw him.

'Food, you know, we all need it!'

'Aye...that'll be great,' he rubbed his hands together. 'Yeah, quite fancy a Chinese.'

'Curry and rice?'

'Fine.'

'Order it. Then you can tell me what it was you were going to tell me this morning.'

His heart sank. 'Oh, err...Tell you what mam, I'll go and pick it up, much quicker. Yes I'll go now' He jumped up out of his chair so quickly he knocked one of the hated plants over, picking it up he avoided his mother's face knowing she would be wearing a huge frown, and was out in the hallway shrugging into his jacket in seconds.

Back in the sitting room his mother stared at the television and shook her head.

He drove slowly to the nearest Chinese take away, going over and over in his mind, what to say to her, and just as quickly rejecting everything.

'Friggin hell,' he thumped his hand hard on the steering wheel, accidently sounding the horn, and giving an old man and his Yorkshire terrier the fright of their lives. 'Sorry.' He shouted out of the open window. The old man shook his walking stick at him, Carter stopped the car.

'Sorry,' he said, jumping out of the car. 'Really, really sorry. It was a mistake. Are you alright?'

The old man glared at him, and the dog barked. 'Be no thanks to you if I wasn't.' He replied and turning he walked away, the dog kept looking back and barking till they were out of sight.

'Shit...Up yours an 'all friggin dog. Cheeky little twat.' Carter muttered, as he got back in the car.

In the twenty minutes it took for his order to be ready. Carter went over it all again.

Well, it's like this mam...I...I'm.

Shit...Shit...Shit.

Finally he decided that the only thing to do would be to just come right out with it.

What if she hates me? He thought as he got back into his car.

She won't, she's my mother.

She might.

Back outside of his house, he took a deep breath, and with a determined look on his face, marched up the steps and opened the front door.

# CHAPTER FORTY EIGHT

Dev sat in the dark on one of the swings eating a bag of chips, soaked in salt and vinegar, and heavy on the batter. Finished he crumpled the paper into a ball and threw it and an empty can of lager, one of five, onto the slide. His thoughts becoming darker as the alcohol kicked in.

He was about to get up from the swing, when he saw Robbie Lumsdon, with someone who he had never seen before, walking past the park.

Silently he stared at Robbie, the hate burning deep in his eyes.

Why me?

Why not you? He thought.

Unaware of the malice directed at him, Robbie burst out laughing at something his friend said- and Dev's hands closed into tight fists. His jaw was clenched so tightly, the pain ran up each side of his face, but he ignored it. Pain he had grown used to, a long long time ago.

The next moment both Robbie and his friend stopped walking because both of them were laughing so hard they were practically bent double. Dev couldn't ever remember finding anything so funny that you cried laughing; his tears had always been of a very different variety.

This thought enraged Dev even more. His fists clenched, he rose up from the swing and took a step forward.

Still they laughed, but managed to stumble a few steps further.

No. He told himself, don't spoil it now.

Do not spoil it now!

A few deep breaths were all he needed to control himself, then slowly and quietly he slipped into the night.

## CHAPTER FORTY NINE

Kerry turned over in bed again sleep might as well have been on another continent it was so far away. She had tried thinking of good things, her coming trials, and the latest races where she had romped home faster than anyone-she'd even gone into the realms of fantasy where she was the world's latest pop star with huge breasts, a film star even; nothing had worked. She stared at the wall in front of her which was less than four inches from her face, but all she could see in her mind was her phone with the latest dreaded text message.

Bastard!

With a sigh she sat up after a moment she frowned, there was something not quite right. Then it hit her, total silence but that should not be, she shared a bedroom with her sister Claire who was a notorious snorer and a teeth grinder and she couldn't even hear her breath.

She felt the hairs on the back of her neck raise as chills ran up her spine. Someone was watching her.

She knew it.

She could feel it.

'Shit.' She muttered.

Quickly she spun round. In the dark she could just make out a shape facing her, a moment later *she* remembered to breath. Claire was sitting on the side of her bed with her bare feet on the floor, staring at her.

'Fuck it, Claire, you frightened the life outta me, sitting there like something out of a horror film-what the hell are you doing?'

Claire let out a small sob.

'What?' Kerry quickly jumped from her bed to Claire's. 'What is it Claire?'

Nearly two years ago Claire, along with some other girls had been kidnapped, and kept captive for most of the time on a boat, they were rescued just in time by Northumbria police led by D I Lorraine Hunt. Since then the whole family had been very protective of her.

Slowly Claire held her phone up. Taking it from her, her own hands trembling slightly as her body filled with dread, Kerry stared at the screen.

'I'm watching you.'

'Bastard!' Kerry threw the phone onto the bed then sat next to Claire, putting her arm around her, she said. 'It's not just you Claire I've been getting the same message all day.'

Claire gasped. 'Have you?'

Kerry nodded slowly.

'Do you...Do you think it might be those new people across the road?'

Kerry frowned. 'But why?'

Claire sighed. 'I don't know,' she looked up at Kerry. 'I can't go through it again.'

'You won't have to. I'm here. Trust me I'll find out who the twat is.'

Claire clung onto Kerry. 'Should...Should we tell the coppers?'

'Not sure, what can they do?'

'They might be able to trace it, the other phone I mean.' She dried her eyes with the back of her hand.

'You think so?'

'Aye, they can do that sort of thing.'

'Right, we'll go up to the cop shop in the morning, but let's not tell mam.'

'Okay.' Claire managed a small smile.

Holding tightly on to each other, the sister's slowly fell into a deep sleep.

## CHAPTER FIFTY

Fiona sighed with relief when she heard the knock on the door; quickly she hurried down the hallway and opened the door to DI Stella Hawkes.

'What took you so long?' She demanded, looking at her watch. The small hand was on twelve and the long hand on six. 'Jesus Christ, It's friggin well more than three hours since I rang and told you that neither of them were back yet.' For a moment she looked over the top of DI Hawkes head, at the black night showing only a few stars.

'Are you going to let me in?'

Fiona transferred her gaze from the sky to DI Hawkes. 'I'm going out of my fucking mind with worry here trying to keep everything from the children...It's not easy when they keep asking for their father. And I think Oliver suspects something... In fact, I'm certain he does.'

'I'm very sorry Fiona, but we had to put a search out. These things do take time.'

'And?' She asked hopefully, finally stepping briskly to one

side to let DI Hawkes in.

Instead of answering, DI Hawkes grabbed Fiona, embraced her and they kissed.

When they broke apart, Fiona said. 'I love you Stella, but he's my husband and the father of my children. I need to know.'

'Nothing... Sorry.' Stella replied closing and double locking the door before following Fiona into the sitting room. 'They were last seen on a CT camera at nine thirty this morning.'

Fiona sank into her settee. Her voice quivering she said. 'But...But where can they be Stella...You promised me, you did. You said they would be safe.'

'If they had stuck to the rules then they would have been fine.' Stella replied. 'Cuppa tea would be nice, oh and have you got any of those chocolate biscuits left, I certainly need a sugar fix. After the day I've had.'

Gritting her teeth, Fiona went into the kitchen and reappeared five minutes later, with two cups on a lemon flowery tray, and a plate of biscuits, that she hated but kept on tap for Stella.

'Look,' Stella said taking one of the cups from Fiona. 'Is there something you're not telling me, something your husband and his brother are involved in?'

'No,' Fiona shook her head in puzzlement. 'Why the hell would there be?'

'You sure about that?'

'For fuck's sake,' Fiona said adamantly. 'Your police woman brain has everyone guilty of something,' she glared at Stella. 'Is everyone guilty of something?'

'Why did they both go against orders?'

'It was business, I already told you, they were meeting an American, it was a very important business meeting that couldn't wait, and they swore they would be careful.'

'Well, obviously they haven't been careful enough, we now have two missing men who are crucial to the case. A case we have been working on for a while now.'

Close to tears, Fiona sighed. 'I don't know what to do. What can I say...I'm sorry.'

Stella stood up and walked over to Fiona, she put her arm across her shoulder. 'We are looking for them Fiona, I do promise you this. In fact their whereabouts are top priority.'

Trembling, Fiona patted the back of Stella's hand.

To take Fiona's mind away from her husband, Stella went on. 'Anyhow, how is Liam?'

Fiona lifted her head and looked into Stella's eyes. 'That's the only bit of good news today. Ten o clock tonight they said he was finally stable, not out of the woods yet, but stable,' she sighed. 'At least it's something.'

'It certainly is.'

Fiona gave a weak smile and held her crossed fingers up. 'My boy is going to make it.'

'Well thank God for that.' Stella smiled.

For a moment both women stared at each other. 'What am I going to do?'

'Be brave Fiona, like you have until now. One thing I need from you though.'

'What's that?'

'The name of the American.'

Fiona hesitated a moment before asking. 'Why?'

'To see if he's missing too.'

'Oh, I never thought. Mr...Mr Plaxton, yes that's it.'

'Had your husband or his brother met Mr Plaxton in person before?'

'I'm not sure. You know I have very little to do with the business side of things.'

'First name?'

Fiona shook her head. 'Don't know...Might be something on John's lap top.'

'Alright, I'm going to make a phone call. Is his lap top here by any chance? Or has he got it with him?'

'Yes, it's here- upstairs, I'll get it.'

When Fiona went upstairs, Stella took out her phone, she went to the window. Parked a few yards away from the front gate an unmarked patrol car flashed its lights when the driver saw the curtains swish open twice. The prearranged signal meant that everything was fine outside.

Although outwardly calm Stella was actually foaming, the whole case had been one big cock up from start to finish. Fiona's husband and brother in law should never have been left to do basically whatever they wanted too. There should have been a trained guard with them at all times, not a newbie, who didn't have a clue.

For fucks sake, Steel, a lot of this is down to you, you and your fucking huge ego, and you are not going to talk your way out of this one. Smooth talking bastard that you are.

Not this time!

No way. He can blame what the hell he likes on cut backs this is still bad policing, whichever way you fucking want to look at it. And- in more ways than one.

She went into the kitchen, opened the window and lit a cigarette. She and Steel went back a long way, she knew he had been responsible for something that had resulted three years ago in one of her very good friends taking the blame for his silly mistakes. Unable to take the backlash, that very good friend had committed suicide, believing that she had been to blame for the death of a small child, when really it had all been down to Steel's stupid incompetence.

Well enough, no more, and you can flash your fucking big teeth at whoever you want, it's not gonna work this time.

Still angry, Stella stubbed her cigarette out and made her call. A minute later she put her phone back in her pocket just as Fiona came back downstairs, carrying a black lap top.

'Right, let's see.' She took the laptop from Fiona.

A few minutes later, she said. 'So, it's Mr David Plaxton, of Hunter Enterprises...Yes?'

'Sounds about right.' Fiona said.

'Okay.' Stella got her phone back out of her pocket. 'I'll pass the information on, and we'll see what time he landed- and which hotel he's booked into. If he's actually in his hotel, it shouldn't take too long.'

Not knowing what to say, Fiona nodded, then stifled a yawn.

'If you want to go to bed, it's fine.'

'No, I'm tired but I doubt sleep will come, until I find out what's gone on with them. Plus we can't sleep together, what if one of them,' she raised her eyes to the ceiling, 'walked in. I would die, how would I ever face them again.'

'I didn't mean we should sleep together...Fiona, when are you going to tell him?'

'I can't...He must never know. We decided this in the beginning, if you remember.' She punched the arm of the settee. 'Where the fuck are they?'

Stella shook her head, what Fiona had just said, was not what she had wanted to hear.

'So basically that's it. It's taken for this to happen for you to realise it's your husband you love and not me.'

'Oh Stella.' Fiona reached out for her, but Stella moved away.

'So what you're saying is what we have...had is over.'

'No that's not what I want.'

Stella laughed. 'Talk about having your cake and eating it, well fuck you madam I'm nobody's bit on the side...And you know what? I'd rather spend the night in the fucking car.'

Fiona stood up. 'That's not what I meant Stella, honestly.'

Ignoring her, Stella put her coat on and left, leaving Fiona to collapse back on the settee feeling more wretched than ever.

Outside Stella went up to the patrol car, spoke a few words to the officer, before making her way over to her own car.

Half an hour later she pulled up outside of a hotel in Newcastle centre. The woman on the night desk, not expecting any guests at this late hour looked at Stella suspiciously as she walked across the red carpeted foyer to her desk. She relaxed slightly when Stella showed her badge.

'DI Stella Hawkes...I believe you have a Mr David Plaxman staying here?'

The receptionist looked at her books, after a moment she lifted her head and nodded. 'He arrived last night, I was on duty, but I've not seen him since.'

'You have a spare key I presume, for his room.'

'Well...yes but.'

'Don't worry we'll knock first.'

The receptionist pressed a button under the counter, a few seconds later a tall black man appeared from behind a door at the back of the counter.

'Take over Jake please, while I go up to a room.'

'Yeah, no bother.' The man smiled at Stella.

A few minutes later they stepped out of the lift.

And I wonder how much a room in here costs, probably more than a whole week's pay. Stella thought, as they walked along the corridor, again the carpet was red, and so thick, that Stella thought they glided rather than walked. The room they wanted was the fourth one down from the lift.

Stella knocked on the door, waited a moment then knocked again, this time louder. After knocking a third time she motioned with her hand for the receptionist to open the door.

The girl slipped the key card into the slot and the door opened. 'Hello, Mr Plaxman.' Stella said loudly, then again before moving into the room. It only took her a few moments to see that the room had not been used, the bed had not been slept in the white towels unused and still on the towel rail. Plus, a full looking holdall lay at the foot of the bed.

She opened the zipper. Inside everything was neatly packed. On the top was a pair of blue pyjamas.

'Well, he never slept in these last night.'

The receptionist shook her head. 'It's not looking good, is it?'

'No it isn't. I'll be wanting to see your CT footage of the last forty eight hours in the morning.'

'Certainly,' the girl closed the door behind them. 'I'll let Jake know.'

Stella headed for home and much needed sleep, she was still feeling raw at Fiona's rejection, and could not get her former lover out of her mind.

Slamming the door behind her she walked up the stairs to her flat, spent the next hour staring at the ceiling, before falling into a deep but troubled sleep.

# CHAPTER FIFTY ONE

Slowly Len crept down the stairs, being extra careful not to wake his daughter up, the last thing he wanted was for her to know where he was going; he would never hear the last of it.

She has a bigger gob on her than her mother, God rest her soul, ever had.

He lifted his right foot high as he stepped over the third step from the bottom, the one that always creaked. He must remember to ask Jacko to take a look at it, he reminded himself for the umpteenth time.

He slipped his shoes on checking that the laces were tied identically, and that his socks-black with large yellow triangles-matched, because he had a similar pair of socks only with smaller triangles, which he's mixed up before.

Then changing his mind, he went into the kitchen, took his shoes off placed them neatly side by side, and took his wellington boots out of the cupboard, deciding that he just didn't have time to sort his thicker socks out, anyhow, surely his legs wouldn't get chaffed in an hour or so, he slipped the wellies on, nearly tripping over in his haste he just managed to catch a cup as he knocked it with his elbow off the bench.

Heaving a sigh of relief, because no way could he have gone out without tidying the mess up the cup would have made, he placed it carefully in the sink and tiptoed the best he could in wellingtons, along the hallway. Then quietly opened his front door and looked up, then down the street, and repeated the action a moment later. Good, he nodded with satisfaction not a soul in sight, although you could just about guarantee at this time of night, anyone out there would defo be up to no good.

Closing and locking the door behind him, he reached the gate and paused for a moment, then went back and checked that he had really locked the door. Satisfied he silently moved up the street towards his cousin Danny's house.

He was about to open the gate when he was grabbed from behind, nervous at the best of times, especially in the middle of the night when he'd practically been forced by his daughter to watch a horror film concerning zombie's, Len screamed.

'Shh you daft sod, it's only me.'

'Fucking idiot!'

'Now- now, Len.' Adam grinned, then imitating Lens voice, went on. 'Is there really need for such fucking bad language? I mean come on- shocking.'

'Very funny.'

'I know.'

'Okay enough you'll have the whole bloody street up.' Jacko moved past them.

Len nearly jumped out of his skin at the sound of Jacko's deep voice, which somehow seemed deeper in a whisper.

Turning to follow him Adam said, 'Where the hell did you spring from?'

'Never mind, you ready for this?'

'Not really.'

'Me neither.' Len moaned.

Jacko shrugged. 'Well...'

Danny came out of his front door and hissed. 'For God's sake you're like a bunch of gibbering old women. You'll have the whole friggin street up in a minute...Tits!'

Adam and Len climbed into the back of the van while Jacko jumped into the front. As Jacko swung the door shut Adam raised his fist in the air and said. 'Okay, let's do this.'

'What did he just say?' Danny asked, looking sideways at Jacko.

'You don't want to know...So, got enough gear?'

Danny nodded as he squeezed the van between two parked cars. 'I swear there's more cars on this friggin estate each and every day, I ask you, is there need to double park like that? Bunch of friggin morons.'

'There's been fucking hell on between that lot, since their young'un got a car; they used to be good friends an' all at one time like.' Adam said.

'Be an even bigger fall out if Steve ever found out that the same young'un was knocking his wife off.' Danny nodded looking at Adam through his rear view mirror as they reached Newbottle.

'No way!' Jacko's jaw dropped open. 'Them two, friggin hell, unbelievable.'

'I don't believe it.' Len shook his head.

Adam shrugged as Danny drove through Philadelphia. 'Doesn't surprise me one little bit, he's always been a horny little bastard, known that for years.'

Jacko turned and looked at Adam. 'You haven't like?'

'Oh dear.' Len stared at Adam.

'What?' Adam blustered. 'No...No not me. What do you take me for, a bloody idiot, when it all comes out there'll be murder on. You all know what Steve's like if he's crossed. Even farmer Mackintire wouldn't have a look in and that bastard's the fucking anti Christ.'

Len pulled a face. 'Huh.'

Danny and Jacko looked at each other with raised eyebrows,

as Danny took the exit to Penshaw village. Five minutes later they were parked outside of a large field at the back of the Monument. Jumping down from the van, Danny went round to the back of the van and got the shovels, handing them out, he said. 'Here you go, and remember perfect squares.'

'What the?' Adam looked at the shovel in his hands with disbelief.

'It's a shovel.' Danny frowned his puzzlement at Adam. 'What do you think it is?'

'I know it's a shovel wanker, what's it for?'

'What the hell do you think it's for, dopey twat?'

'Aye that.'

'What?'

Jacko burst out laughing, while Len stood with his jaw unhinged.

Slowly Danny shook his head. 'You thought I meant fucking dope didn't you.'

'Well you did say grass, never thought you meant,' he gestured towards the field. 'That sort of friggin grass.'

'Unbelievable.'

'Oh he's that alright, I might be hard up and parish damned like me mother used to say, but I'm not and never will be, a fucking low life drug dealer.' Jacko shook his head.

'Me neither.' Len said, with conviction.

'Well when you said Farmer Mackintire, you know, I just sort of assumed, that's all. Everybody knows he's a bit dodgy like...Well, just about everybody.'

'So the old sod grows the shit?' Jacko nodded. 'Makes sense now, it wasn't fucking bunny rabbits youse two had been after that night you hopped home bullock naked, was it?'

Adam looked at the ground and slowly shook his head, while Len and Danny both with pretty much the same picture in their minds again of Adam hopping home naked. Burst out laughing.

After a few minutes, Danny wiped his eyes and shushing the others, handed the rest of the shovels out. 'Right, let's get on with it, got no time to mess about.'

One by one as they collected their shovels they walked into the field of cultivated grass.

Len was still chuckling at Adam. 'Okay, keep it down.' Danny said. 'We don't want the old creep out here with his fucking gun do we now?'

'Very funny.' Adam pulled a face as he measured the width of his stretch out.

An hour later they were back home and loading the rolls of grass into Len's garden.

Any one fancy another trip?' Danny asked.

'You're off your fucking rocker mate. We're lucky we got away with this lot. Trust me the old twat must be having his once a fucking year sleep.' Adam shook his head.

'He's right like.' Jacko agreed. 'I had visions the whole time of farmer Mackintire chasing us all bollock naked, home like.'

'Fuck off.' Adam retorted, while the others laughed.

'Anyhow, we can't cos there's no more room in me garden, is there?' Len frowned.

'Well, just saying like. And there's a few more than farmer Mackintire who grows grass around here.'

'Aye there's him over Finkle Abby way.' Jacko said. 'But no way. I'm off to bed.'

'Me as well.' The others echoed as they went their separate ways, leaving Danny scowling at them.

## CHAPTER FIFTY TWO

She crept into the corner and pulled an old sack over her weary body. Staring into the blackness, she sighed. Never had she thought she would end up in a place like this, in some God forsaken third world country maybes, but not in England, never in England. Not her, she had a life, a good decent life. Things like this just didn't happen to the people where she came from.

Never.

The tears came again, as they did every night. As usual she brushed them away.

Like a child she put her thumb in her mouth and sucked, trying to ease the pain from a throbbing cut. She felt ill, her head was aching and she shivered knowing at this time of night she had no chance of begging a few pain killers they would all be busy, far too busy.

And what was she to them, just another servant, easily replaceable, a nothing, a nobody. Any one of the slaves in here could do what she did, and they probably wouldn't even notice if she was dead and buried.

Pain, tell them she was in pain, it would only provide more of the nights entertainment for them. The only one, who would ever help in any way and that was when none of the others were around, was old Nick. And he would be fast asleep.

Many ways of escape had haunted her dreams and spilled over into her waking hours, but all had proved impossible. The few who had tried to escape had never made it. The proof was their scalps which she was forced to wash and hang in the kitchen.

The sound of snoring reached her from the other corner. Thank God, she thought. The new kid, God bless her, has managed to fall asleep at last, after crying her heart out for the last four hours. Only she had come in here as a kid, but she was that no more. Her youth gone forever.

Slowly she sat up and looked around.

There were seven women sleeping on the floor tonight, three were yet to come in. Of the seven, four were deadly silent and she guessed that these four were like her, wide awake, again, and staring at the walls. In the morning their sleeping places would be taken by those out working the night.

She heard her name whispered, once, twice and looked quickly to her right. Marta was sitting up staring at her.

'I'm going to do it.' She whispered.

'No Marta.'

'I have to... I can't take it anymore. This is not living this is death, only worse. Delivering babies, then watching as they are snatched from their mothers...No more.'

'Please Marta, no...No, I'm begging you. You know what will happen. No one ever escapes.'

'I would rather be dead, than live another day in here. Already I have lost one child of my own. Where is it?'

Tears ran down her face as she stared at Christina.

'How many more?'

Marta was Rumanian; she had come here over a year ago, with the promise of a job in a hairdressing saloon and a shared flat with another girl, instead she had found herself here. A book of midwifery shoved in her hand and ordered to learn it all by morning.

The other girl Lorna had betrayed her for money and a false promise that she would be free. Like others out of desperation she had fallen for their lies. Instead of walking free in the sunshine with a new life, and cash in her pocket, Lorna was kept in the next room and used constantly, not even allowed to work or mix with the others for fear of reprisals, not allowed to shake a tiny bit of boredom from her days. And her nights, her nights were very long indeed. And although what Lorna had done was wrong on every count Marta still felt a twinge of pity for her, for her life if possible was even worse now.

A scream pulled Christina from her thoughts hastily she sat up, knowing at once where it had come from. The new girl.

'Shh,' she said, quickly. 'If they hear you...'

But the young girl screamed again.

And again, this time she beat her heels on the stone floor, Christina watched as blood started to ooze across the floor.

'I want to go home,' she screamed. 'Let me outta here, now...Now.'

'Shh, please they'll come for you.' The words were barely out of Marta's mouth when the door opened, and he with the scar, the one they all hated the most, came in.

He grabbed the young girl by her hair and dragged her out, slamming the door behind him.

For a long while Christina sat with her head in her hands, wondering if the girl would ever come back. Not for the first time had she sat like this, praying for a young girl to be safe.

## CHAPTER FIFTY THREE

Across town, and long after the sisters had fallen asleep, Lorraine lay staring at the ceiling, her thoughts jumping from the handsome face of the scalped man, to her own problem. Turning over she looked at Luke's sleeping face, she loved him so much, and it wasn't fair the way she was taking things out on him.

She knew this, for God's sake but she had not been able to stop herself.

They had talked for hours after they got back from her mothers, Luke had forgiven her, as deep inside she'd known he would

Why? She asked herself again.

Why can't I just let go?

Quietly she slipped out of bed, going to the window she opened the curtains slightly and stared out at the full moon. It was a few moments later when she noticed just how quiet it was, as if Luke had suddenly stopped breathing, slowly she turned to see Luke sitting up and watching her.

With a sigh she walked back to her side of the bed. Sitting

down with her back to him, she said. 'I know we discussed it Luke, but I want to tell you again, I'm truly sorry, I really shouldn't take it out on you.'

Luke reached over and ran his hand down her arm. 'It's alright Lorry...Okay.'

The next moment Lorraine snuggled up to Luke. He could feel the dampness on his shoulder from her cheek, and was at a loss what to do, knowing he was damned either way he played it.

So instead of saying anything, he just held her tight. After a minute or two he felt her relax against him and he slowly eased her down onto the bed.

'It will soon be over Lorraine, one more day that's all.'

'I know. I know.'

Like the sisters they fell asleep in each other's arms.

## CHAPTER FIFTY FOUR

She sat with her head in her hands, silent tears flowing down her face. The tears were not for her but for her friend Ann, who lay broken and twisted in the corner, having been dragged in an hour ago. And for the new girl Sarah, who was really just a kid at fourteen years old, already condemned to a life of hell, and who had not yet been brought back. Marta sat in the opposite corner, staring at her, a look of pure rebellion on her face. Christina dreaded to think what she was planning.

Her tears were silent but not so those of the newborn, or the heart broken newborns mother, who every now and again screamed as if she was in agony; for her child.

And she was in pain, the pain that only a mother could know.

For a child that would be gone tomorrow as if it had never been, taken out of the country and sold. If it was a boy, chances were it might have a decent life adopted by a childless couple, or simply bought and brought up as their own.

A girl, her prospects were different, she could have the chances that a boy had, but more often than not they were sold into the sex market and kept simply as slaves. She felt a hand on her arm and knew that it was Marta trying to comfort her.

If only she could get out of here, the names she knew, the lives she could save.

If only!

But how, again she wracked her brains for a way out.

For although she had begged others not to take the chance, she now having reached the very end of her limits, realised what they meant when they said they could take no more and would rather be dead.

## CHAPTER FIFTY FIVE

Ten minutes after Jacko and the rest of them, had left Danny's, Adam was on his way back, unknown to him he was being shadowed by Len. He reached out to open the gate and got the shock of his life when someone else's hand, opened it for him. He spun round.

'You fucking idiot, you frightened the shite out of me.'

'Sorry.' Len grinned.

'Please don't do that.'

'What?'

Frightening, he thought, but said, 'Never mind.'

Len shrugged. 'Guess you've come back for more, same as me?'

Adam nodded. 'Wonder if Jacko's changed his mind.'

They both looked up the street, but there was no sign of their friend.

Quietly they crept up the path, both relived to see that the light was still on.

'Should we knock, or just go in?' Len whispered.

'Better try the door first, don't want Danny running scared in case his neighbours hear us. Or wake the wife up, he'll go crazy and that's a fact.'

'They should be in bed this time of a night like...Well its morning really.'

'Aye whatever.'

Adam reached for the door and slowly turned the handle, a moment later he stepped back as the door opened and Danny and Jacko were standing there.

Danny grinned and quickly put his finger to his lips, as he gestured with his other hand for them to move out of the way, quickly they steeped to one side, then followed Jacko and Danny.

A few minutes later they were in the van and heading towards Penshaw Monument.

'Knew you lot would come back.' Danny said.

'Look's like you didn't even go away.' Adam said to Jacko.

'I did, just came back quicker than youse two. Why did youse change your minds?'

'Same reason as you did.'

'Aye,' Jacko laughed. 'Wonder what that is.'

'Money?' Len said.

Behind his back, Adam caught Jacko's eye, pointed to Len's head with his finger and shook his own head. 'Fucking raving nutter.' He mouthed.

'We are only doing one more run though aren't we?' Len looked at Danny.

'Aye that's the plan, you know what they say, in for a penny in for a pound, cos this is the only night we'll be able to do this, unless we cross over into Cumbria. You know what the friggin farmers are like around here, tight knit bunch, once word spreads about tonight, it'll be all over the friggin north east.'

'Okay, let's do this.' Adam said. While Len looked sideways at him.

An hour later with twenty rolls in the back of the van they decided to call it a night.

PART TWO

## 24 HOURS PREVIOUSLY

Twin brothers John and Martin were drinking coffee in a cafe in the centre of Newcastle. Handsome, medium build, dark haired and green eyed, the only way you could tell them apart was that John wore a black suit and Martin a grey one, both wore grey ties. Plus the small hardly noticeably scar on the back of John's hand, a scar accidently given to him by his brother when they were seven and learning to play football. A scar John relentlessly waved in Martin's face whenever he wanted him to do something that Martin did not agree with.

A man neither of them knew, dark and swarthy with a scar on his face, and certainly not resembling the one they were waiting for, passed by, then suddenly turned and pulled a chair close up to Martin, the next thing Martin felt was something hard digging into his ribs-with a look of horror, he stared at his brother.

'What?' John asked.

Struck dumb with fright, Martin could only stare at John, the man answered for him. 'He has a gun in his ribs. If you don't do as I say right now, I promise you, I will shoot the fucker.'

John's face turned white. 'No...I mean...Yes. What do you

want?'

'Stand up and walk in front of me, at the bottom of the steps, there is a white van, get into the back.'

For a moment John was frozen solid, his heart pounding.

'Now.'

The command when it was delivered shocked him into standing up. Slowly staring in front of him, he walked past his terrified brother, headed down the steps and climbed into the van. The door was held open by a scowling bald headed man, with bulging biceps.

A few seconds later he was joined in the back of the van by Martin, who was pushed so hard from behind him that he fell to the floor lying spread eagled for a moment. John helped his brother up, glaring at the man with the gun who had climbed in behind him.

'What...What do you want?' John asked, as Martin stared at him, willing him to shut up.

The man laughed. 'Oh I think you already know that...Your assured silence.'

'You've got it.' Martin quickly said.

Looking at him, then at the man with the gun, John nodded. 'Anything you want.'

The man smiled. 'We've got it alright. We know where your wife and children are.'

John's face turned from white to a sickly green, a moment later he vomited over the man's shoes.

'You dirty stinking bastard.' The man jumped back, then lurched forward and hit John over the head with the butt of his gun. John collapsed onto the floor.

'No.' Martin yelled as the man went to hit John again.

Pulling back the man glared at him, he stepped forward and leaned over Martin, his left hand steadying him as the van gained speed.

'What are you going to do?'

The man laughed, and put his gun away. 'Don't fret, after your silence is assured and the trial is thrown out of court, we walk away and you and your brother will be forgotten about.'

He kicked John on the side of his head.

'No.' Martin yelled.

Grinning at him, he kicked John again.

MONDAY

## CHAPTER FIFTY SIX

He blinked as he stared into the blackness, not knowing if it was night or day, wondering how he had managed to fall asleep, amazing, he thought, then his mind latched onto the song *Amazing Grace,* As the song went round and round in his head he feared he was going mad.

To save himself he concentrated on the past, thinking of summers long gone, days on the beech spent with his family, fights with his brother John their mother parting them, demanding that they be friends, her terrible attempts at cooking food that even the dog turned his nose up at. His Father's wonderful meals, he had been a pastry chef in a large hotel, he remembered how John was going to follow in his footsteps, but instead changed his mind and they set up in business together.

The sweet smell of autumn then winter nights by the fire huddled together on the huge leather settee. Christmas holidays, Easter holidays, summer days at the seaside. But thoughts fly quickly and soon he had gone through a life time of memories. And once more the tears started to flow.

Martin had never married, who would mourn his passing, the old folks were long gone, not even a maiden aunt left all he had was his brother John, his brother's wife Fiona and his nephews and niece.

And his last memory rose, as if it had been waiting in line, o the bald headed man saying. ''We will forget all about you.''

He knew now exactly what he had meant by that.

## CHAPTER FIFTY SEVEN

Carter crept down the stairs, he'd stood for a moment with his ear pressed to his mother's door, but he couldn't hear anything, he could only hope as his foot reached the last stair that she was still asleep. Deciding to grab something on the way into work rather than eat here, he shrugged his jacket on checking that he had his badge this time, even though Luke had sorted the ticket for him, he didn't want it to happen again, not with that miserable traffic warden. He reached for the front door handle.

'Morning son, I've made you a lovely bacon sandwich and a nice cuppa tea.'

Carter's shoulders slumped as he groaned loudly.

'What?'

'Nothing, nothing...I'm in a hurry, don't think I've got time for breakfast this morning mother. Really, thanks though, you enjoy yours mind you.'

'Nonsense, everybody needs a good breakfast inside of them especially policemen, or police women. The job you do, you all need your energy. Now come on in here son.'

It was the smell of the breakfast cooking that lured him on. 'What the hell is she being so nice for?' He muttered as he made his way along to the kitchen.

'Okay son sit down,' his mother said as she put a plate of bacon, eggs, beans and mushrooms on the table. 'Toast?'

Looking at the food Carter totally caved in, he smiled. 'Please.'

He was halfway through his meal when he realised that his mother was sitting opposite, staring at him.

'Okay, spit it out.'

'What, the bacon?'

'Don't be funny, you know what I mean, you have something to tell me,' she waved his car keys at him. 'And you are not getting your mitts on these until you do.'

Carter's heart sank. He put his knife and fork on his plate as he swallowed the last piece of egg.

Aw shit, what the hell can I say? He thought, buying time by wiping his mouth with a tissue.

'Come on, we haven't got all day...Well, I have, but you have to get to work. Don't you?'

He took a deep breath and was just about to speak, when the post man dropped letters through the door. Jumping up Carter said, 'I'll get them.'

Quickly he left the kitchen, walked along the hallway and scooped half a dozen letters up.

Great, he thought looking at the envelopes as he made his way back, Gas and electric bills, that'll keep her occupied.

'Here mam,' he put the pile in front of her. 'Bills, more bills, junk mail, and what looks like a letter from aunt Pat.'

She picked the assortment up and silently flicked through them, as Carter put his jacket on, then held out his hand for his keys.

'Sit down'

'No mother I'm going to be late.'

She shook her head. 'Something's bothering you son and I wouldn't be calling myself much of a mother if I don't find out what it is.'

He sat down and glared at her. 'I'm not six years old anymore mother!'

It was probably the closest Carter had ever come in his life to losing his temper; he felt the urge to bang his fist on the table and was close to giving into it when his phone rang.

Snatching it out of his pocket he looked at the caller I D. 'It's the boss mother, I've got to go, now.'

'Alright son. I'll still be here tonight.'

## CHAPTER FIFTY EIGHT

'Are you sure you don't want me to come to court with you Lorry?' Mavis asked, as Lorraine came in with the dog.

Hanging Duke's leader on a peg on the back of the kitchen door, Lorraine shook her head. 'No mam, I just want it over and done with, plus I've got a another case to attend, so I'll be in Durham most of the day.'

'As long as you're sure pet.'

Lorraine kissed her mother's cheek. 'I'm sure mam.'

On her way down the path to her car, Lorraine's phone rang, pausing a moment she pulled it out and put it to her ear.

'You what?' she practically yelled. 'Friggin hell, I'll be there in five.'

Her plan had been to go home and change into a smart black trouser suit with a white blouse, instead there was no time, white trainers, blue jeans and lilac jumper would have to do.

The court could like it or lump it!

Jumping in the car, she used a hairbrush she kept in the glove compartment and tied her hair up in a pony tail. When this was over if she could get back home in time to change for court, she would, but it wasn't looking good.

She shrugged, as she reversed out of her mother's yard. 'Fuck it, they'll have to take me as I come!'

Reaching the station five minutes later, she quickly hurried inside opening the office door she saw, Carter, Dinwall, and Sanderson, more or less standing in a line, each with a worried look on their face.

'Okay, someone's been found dead don't for God's sake tell me it's another scalping?'

Sanderson nodded. 'Not sure yet, we've been told that her head is covered in blood...Young girl, found between Marsdon and Seaburn.'

'Shit...Near to where the last body was found?'

'Close enough.'

'Please don't tell me it was a member of the public who found her?'

'It was, a young man, name of Davy Lockheart, and the fucking idiot only went and phoned the Sunderland Echo, and a pile of his mates before he phoned us.'

'What!'

'Yes.' Dinwall put in. 'Crime scene wrecked. A squad car from Sunderland, just happened to be passing, and he's keeping the people who gathered there at bay.'

'Oh for fucks sake...Please say he has not taken photo's and spread them on that bloody internet?'

'Not that we know of boss.' Dinwall went on. 'I've checked a few sites, nothing showing up.'

'I'll kill the git if he has, frigging moron.'

Just then Luke walked in, he was carrying Lorraine's black suit on a coat hanger with her blouse, and the other things she would need in a carrier bag. 'Thought you might want these?'

'Thanks Luke.' she ran her hand up his arm as she took the coat hanger from him. 'Give me five minutes to change then we'll all head to Seaburn.'

They reached Seaburn half an hour later to find DI Stella Hawkes talking to a young man.

'What's she doing here?' Luke said.

Lorraine shook her head, briefly wondering if there was something going on that she hadn't been told about.

'Obviously that's the guy who found the body.' She muttered to Luke.

Putting a smile on she walked up to them followed by her four officers. 'Hello.'

DI Hawkes looked up. 'Hi, I was passing when it came over

he radio so thought I'd better step in. This is Davy Lockheart, he found the body.'

'He also informed the press,' Lorraine snapped, waving her arm at three press photographers. 'Put those cameras away now, or I'll have you all in court for obstructing the law.' She shouted as she spun round to face them.

Quickly they put their cameras down and stepped back.

'I already told them,' Stella said.

'Took a hell of a lot of notice, didn't they.' Lorraine glared at the photographers.

Turning back she looked at Davy Lockheart, who she noted was nearly as ginger as Carter.

'Well?' She demanded.

He blushed. 'Sorry, don't know what I was thinking of.'

'If you would like to wait here or go sit in the police car, the choice is yours, which ever I will need to talk to you.' She turned to Stella. 'Where's the body?'

'Come with me.'

Turning back, Lorraine said to Carter. 'Wait with him and do not let him use his phone,' then to Luke. 'With me, youse two,' she flung over her shoulder to Sanderson and Dinwall, 'do a search of the immediate area.'

'Yes boss.' They echoed.

As they walked away, Dinwall said to Sanderson, 'She's not a happy bunny, about Hawkes is she? I mean it is strange how she keeps turning up all of a sudden isn't it though.'

Dinwall stopped walking. 'I know,' he looked over his shoulder, 'she's the scalper.'

'Yeah very funny.'

Lorraine, Stella and Luke walked over to the beech hut; the back of the hut was facing them, just before they walked round to the front Lorraine groaned.

'What?' Stella asked.

'That's all we need.'

Coming down the road towards them, was the mobile BBC news van.

'Quick Luke, don't let them within twenty yards,' she looked round. 'Where the hell is the ambulance and Scottie?'

'Jesus Christ.'

Lorraine swung her head back to Stella. Then to where Stella was looking at. Her heart sank immediately; the body sprawled on the bench looked to be that of a girl of about fourteen to fifteen years old. Her hair covered in blood hung down her back, from what could be seen of her face at this angle it was drenched in blood. More blood was dripping from the wooden bench to the stone path.

Please. Lorraine thought, not another one, not with this friggin circus gathering.

Then she remembered a young girl had been reported missing late last night when she had failed to come home. A description had been given but at this moment it was impossible to tell.

Please don't let this be her.

Scottie and his team arrived a few minutes later, at the same time a patrol car with four police constables pulled up.

After saying a quick hello to Scottie, and as he covered the crime scene with a white tent, she sent the police officers on a finger tip search of the area.

'Any conclusions yet?' He was looking at Lorraine but it was Stella who answered him.

'I only got here a few minutes ago, and concentrated on keeping people at bay with the PC. Really this is the first proper look I've had of the victim.'

Lorraine shrugged, fully suited up she followed Scottie into the tent. As they looked down at the body, Lorraine breathed a sigh of relief. 'You thinking the same as me Scottie?'

'I guess so. Although at first glance, given the ongoing enquiries, this could be mistaken for a scalping, it most definitely isn't. Also, it didn't happen here. Not enough blood splatter.'

'I know,' Lorraine stepped closer. 'Looks like she's had one or two severe blows to her head.'

'Well she's either crawled here, or she's been carried.'

Lorraine's phone rang. Caller ID said Luke. 'Yes Luke?'

'I'm on my way up Lorraine. Think we've found the murder weapon.'

'Okay.' Shoving her phone into her pocket Lorraine told Scottie what Luke had said.

A few minutes later Luke entered the tent, in his hands he had a skateboard. 'I found it at the bottom of the hill near the car park, there's also quite a lot of blood at the same spot on the corner of the wall so, I'm thinking it's more than likely the poor kid's had an accident.'

'Well if she's been going down the bank at some speed, and you know how sharp the corner of brick walls are.' Scottie said, handing Luke a large plastic bag for the skate board.

'Bless her,' Lorraine shook her head. 'We'll check the board for prints, but I think we're on the right track defo an accident.'

Scottie's team transferred the girl onto a stretcher. 'I'll check for brick dust as soon as we get back.'

'Right, we have to be moving. 'I'll call sometime this afternoon Scottie.'

Outside she said to Stella. 'Could you please go with Scottie, and see if we can get identification, we have to be at Durham rown in less than an hour.

'No problem.'

'Thank you...Oh, after you deal with that lot first.' Lorraine ooked in the direction of the television cameras.

'Yes, consider it done.'

## CHAPTER FIFTY NINE

Fiona insisted on walking Molly to school, even though she ha
kicked up a big fuss, demanding that she was allowed to walk ther
with her new friend Suzy. They were at their gate as Suzy came ou
of her gate and skipped across the road towards them. 'Hello, loo'
what I've got.' Holding out her hand she showed them a brigh
shiny fifty pence piece. Then opened her mouth and with he
finger, showed them a gap in her teeth at the side.

'Nearly the last one and mam still thinks I believe in fairies
As if,' she raised her eyes skywards. 'We can get some sweets a
the shop on the way.'

Fiona frowned at her. Her tone was harsh as she snapped
'Really child, and lose more teeth. And we don't need an escort.'

Molly dug her nails in her mother's hand as Suzy stoppe
dead. 'I was only going to walk with you.' Her lip started to quive
as she stared wide eyed at Fiona.

Molly let go of her mother's hand and moved forward
grabbing Suzy's hand, she said. 'Come on.' Suzy brightened u
and together they headed up the street towards the school.

Feeling totally wretched, Fiona followed them. Fuck, she thought, fancy taking it out on a small child. How horrible am I. I'll have to make it up to her somehow.

'Hello girls and good morning.' Mr Skillings said, from Vanessa's garden as they passed.

'Hi Mr Skillings,' both girls said, as they waved.

Mr Skillings nodded at Fiona, she returned the nod with a barely noticeable smile.

Coming out of her house holding two cups of tea, Vanessa had noticed the exchange. 'What a miserable bitch.' She said, handing Mr Skillings cup of tea over.

'Aye she seems that way, wonder if there's anything in that, you know, on the run business?'

'No, daft bugger, it's just kids talk.'

'Aye, that might be, but the adults are talking about it as well. Tell you what, why don't you ask her if she wants a cuppa when she comes back, she might be a bit lonely, you know being new and all that.'

Fiona watched Molly and Suzy go into school, she sighed pleased now that Molly had made a friend, and that she looked quite happy to be going to school.

And isn't that a first! Disgusted with herself for being nasty to Suzy. Who on the short journey to school had really seemed like a nice little girl, with a lovely smile. She turned away and slowly headed back home, when she reached her house, the man next door, who was in the garden across the road shouted over. 'Fancy a cuppa pet?'

For a moment Fiona was in shock, a perfect stranger inviting her for a cup of tea.

Then with another sigh she thought. Why not? It's better than being alone.

She crossed the road. With a brave smile she said. 'Yes please.'

## CHAPTER SIXTY

acko decided to walk along to the Grasswell shop for the
Sunderland Echo after dropping Melanie off at school, though
these days she much preferred to walk there with her friends, but it
gave him something to do, sort of a kick start on a morning, plus
his mind was content that she was safe as he watched her walk
through the school gates.

He had just passed where the old railway bridge used to be at
Grasswell, when he heard a noise, turning his head he saw the thug
who went by the name of Dev.

What the hell.

Dev had Mrs. Holland's cat in his hands and he looked about
to strangle it.

'Hey, what the hell are you doing?' Jacko quickly crossed the
road as Dev threw the cat on the wall, it crouched there hackles up,
watching them.

In fact Dev had found the cat limping, his intention had been
to open the gate and put the cat in the yard, but he knew this
bastard wouldn't believe him, so instead he yelled. 'Nowt to do

with you.'

'That's old Mrs. Holland's cat, you moron.'

'So what, the old bugger's batty as a fruit cake, she'll not eve
miss the fucking ugly thing.'

By now Jacko was eye to eye with Dev.

'That batty old woman as you call her, had five kids, four wer
burned to death in a house fire, the other one died a canny fe
years back, the cat is all she has.' He reached for Dev's throat, bu
Dev knew how strong Jacko was and quickly jumped back.

But Jacko was just as quick, and was only a step away whe
he yelled in Dev's face. 'Yes run you fucking low life coward, bu
before you do, know this, she thinks her son is still alive, but reall
he's a copper who visits regular. So just watch it creep, cause i
anything happens to that cat it's *you*, the copper and me will b
looking for.'

Back peddling Dev stuck his middle finger up at Jacko, befor
quickly turning, and just short of a run he headed up the back all
towards Houghton.

His body shaking with anger, Jacko repeatedly punched hi
left hand. Shaking his head and all thoughts of his newspape
forgotten, not trusting himself, he went in the other direction t
Dev, up Cellar Hill terrace towards Newbottle and the othe
entrance to Melanie's school. Trying hard to throw a smile a

people he knew as he passed them, though guessing rightly that his smile looked like anything but. He breathed in deeply as he headed up the bank, willing himself to calm down.

Walking past the school he glanced at the empty yard, all quiet now he thought, silent as the grave.

He didn't see Adam hurrying down the bank on the other side of the road, who on spotting Jacko had broke out into a near run.

'Hey.' The shout startled Jacko; he looked in the direction just as Adam ran across the road, barely managing to beat a bus on its way up the bank. The bus driver sounded his horn as Adam jumped onto the path in front of Jacko.

'Bloody idiot, feeling suicidal today or what?'

Adam grinned. 'Got some great news.'

'Worth dying for, is it?'

'Just listen, for fuck's sake...You're starting to sound more like that old fart Len, every day.'

'I'll old fart you in a minute.'

'Right, okay, sorry. Just listen...Farmer Mackintire is away in Spain, has been for a week, and there for another two, him and the whole fucking clan.' He grinned at Jacko.

'And?'

'And...It means we can go back there tonight, yes!'

'You reckon.'

'Aye, why not?'

'Because thicko, where the hell are we gonna store the grass?'

'Oh...Never thought about that.'

'You never do,'

'Anyhow Danny might have sold it already.'

'Doubt that.'

'Have you seen him this morning?'

'Not yet.'

'Good, we'll call round then, fingers crossed.' He fell into step with Jacko and they walked to the crossroads at Newbottle, turned left and headed towards the Seahills.

Five minutes later they were knocking on Danny's door just as a lorry pulled up. The driver a think set man wearing dark blue overalls, greying frizzy hair tied at the back, and with no front teeth, nodded at them.

Just then Danny came out of the door and gave the driver a wave. 'That's the last lot gone and not ten o clock yet,' he said to Jacko and Adam as he rubbed his hands together. 'Told you it was a good idea.'

'Spot on.' Adam said. 'And I've got great news.'

He tried to tell Danny about Farmer Mackintire as they walked back up the path, but Danny was too busy smiling at 'no teeth,' too listen properly.

After talking to the lorry driver, the three of them jumped into Danny's van and they drove up to Len's allotment with the lorry following them. On the way Adam told Danny about farmer Mackintire being away.

Danny shrugged, and looked at Jacko. 'Think it's worth the risk mate?'

Jacko heaved a large sigh. 'Not sure.'

'Why aye man,' Adam put in. 'Money for old rope. You get nowt if you don't try.'

'Well, we're quid's in now, but I wouldn't like to think we had to spend our hard earned cash on new clothes. You know what I mean, and Len certainly won't suit the bollock naked look.'

Danny and Jacko burst out laughing, as Adam said. 'Yeah very funny.'

They reached Len's allotment and between them, soon had the lorry loaded. 'Thanks mate.' Danny said as the man handed the money over.

'Nee bother,' he replied in a thick Newcastle accent. 'If you get anymore, you know me number.' He then jumped into the lorry and drove off.

Adam rubbed his hands together as Danny started counting the money out, just as he finished his phone rang.

'Yeah, uh-huh, yeah. Sorry but it's all gone mate...Oh, yeah uh-hu, yeah,' with a huge grin he put his phone in his pocket 'Another client, wants five hundred rolls. More if we can get them Get in.' He punched the air.

'So, we on for tonight then, lads?' Adam asked.

'Might as well. 'Jacko said. 'Got nowt better to do.'

'Oh yes.'

'Right, same time, same place, I'll let our Len know.' Danny turned to go.

'Err, you forgotten something?' Adam said.'

'Just testing.' Danny grinned, before paying them out.

## CHAPTER SIXTY ONE

Vanessa could barely contain her excitement as she heard Sandra tip-tapping up the path, rushing to the door, she practically shouted. 'One more day, that's all just one more bloody day.'

Sandra laughed. 'I'm truly amazed at how you've managed to keep it a secret.'

'Yeah me as well.'

'Cuppa?'

'Not long had one. But help yourself...You'll never guess who we had in the garden for a cuppa earlier this morning.'

'No, could be anyone, knowing you.'

'Cheeky...Just her across the road.'

'Oh aye,' Sandra raised her eyebrows. ' How did that come about?'

'Mr Skillings asked her over. Actually she's alright. Talks a bit posh mind you, a bit toffy nosed. You can tell she's not from round here, but she was nice.'

'Okay I believe you, it takes all sorts, and there's good and bad in their world, same as there is in ours... Any mention of that being a safe house then.'

'No, I didn't ask. I mean, how can you really?'

'Surprise number two.'

Vanessa pulled a face at her friend. 'Anyhow I've invited her to the party tomorrow night, you'll get to meet her and you can ask her yourself.'

'Err, no.'

Vanessa shrugged. 'Well, it's probably rubbish anyhow. But our Darren said there was a strange car parked outside of hers late last night, though there wasn't any cars there when the kids went to school.'

They walked into the sitting room as Sandra was sipping her tea, looking across the road, she said. 'Was it a black car?'

'He didn't say. Why?'

'Cos there's a black one there now, and she's coming down the path with two blokes, who keep looking around, and she doesn't look too happy.'

## CHAPTER SIXTY TWO

Well thankfully that's one down.' Lorraine smiled at Luke outside of Durham county court.

Luke nodded his agreement. 'Another creep off the roads, one more to go...And don't worry, it'll be fine.'

'All we have to pin on him now is his illegal dog fighting, for some reason the thick git thinks we can't go after him for something else, once he's locked up.'

Luke laughed.' Right, but through all of this I've had the feeling that something else is going on with him. Not just what we've got him for, nor the dog fighting...Gut instinct, he's involved with something else.'

About to agree with him, Lorraine threw him a smile as her phone rang. 'What?' she said a moment later.

Shaking her head she put her phone back in her pocket. 'It's not...The young girl with the skate board, It's not Sarah Rose Sinclair.'

'It's not! Shit... I mean good...You know what I mean. So who is it then?''

'Sarah Rose Sinclair's parents have been to the morgue and the girl there is definitely not their daughter.'

'So we still have a missing girl, and also an unknown body.'

'Which means; Sinclaire, may hopefully still be alive...She could be just hiding out somewhere.'

'Her parents did say she had stormed out of the house in the huff, and apparently not for the first time.'

Taking hold of Luke's hand, they walked across the road and down the street to a cafe. Luke ordered coffee and Lorraine a glass of diet coke.

'Do you want anything to eat?' Luke asked. When she didn't answer, he said, 'Lorraine.'

'Sorry?' she looked at him for a moment, then as if realising what he had asked, she said. 'No thanks.'

Reaching across the table Luke took Lorraine's hand. 'It'll soon be over love.'

'I know...And I am truly sorry for the way I've gone on. Don't know how you put up with it this long without losing it. Really don't deserve you.'

'Well of course you don't,' he grinned. 'I'll admit it wasn't easy but it did become easier with a sort of a plan that Mavis and Peggy came up with.'

'You what?'

Luke smiled. 'Sorry love but something had to be done. I had to let you think that things were going to be over with us, trust me it nearly killed me.'

Lorraine shook her head. 'I don't friggin well believe it.'

Staring at her Luke's heart began to sink, expecting lightening to strike at any time he was surprised when she smiled.

'Guess youse did the right thing, then.'

Relived, he smiled as he said. 'Okay if you don't want to eat and as we have an hour to kill, how about a walk along the river side.'

'Sounds good to me.'


Feeling the tension growing in her shoulders and neck, Lorraine walked into the courtroom. And there he was, standing grinning at her behind the partition. It was obvious he had been looking for her.

She fought for control but all she could see was him covered in a blood red shimmering haze. Her hands clenched, she moved forward looking quickly from side to side, for something, anything that would smash the partition.

# CHAPTER SIXTY THREE

The new girl, obviously still in shock at the predicament she found herself in, stood by the kitchen sink her whole body shaking as she stared up at the scalps.

'What are those?' She asked, although she already knew the answer.

'Scalps.' Christina replied.

Earlier, after she had held Sarah for the rest of the night, when she had been dragged back in, Christina had asked for some help with the cleaning, hoping and praying that they would give her Sarah, anything to keep her away as long as possible from what awaited the girl, truly hoping that before that happened she would come up with a safe plan to escape, which would have to be soon before Marta totally lost it and just ran, and because she had already seen most of the men eyeing the girl up.

'Why?' She turned to face Christina.

'A warning.'

'Did...Did they try to run away?'

Christina nodded.

'Is that...Is that why?'

Sarah backed away from the sink, her eyes wide and full of tears. 'What...What?' She folded in on herself and collapsed onto the floor.

Quickly Christina dragged her over to a chair. She lifted her onto the seat and gently stroked the side of Sarah's face. After a moment Sarah opened her eyes. Christina's heart dropped when she saw the depths of sadness and fear starring back at her.

'Is this it?' Sarah whispered.

'No, never give up...I'm trying to think of a way to escape without being caught.'

'Take me with you.' Sarah clutched at Christina's t-shirt. 'Please...Take me with you.'

'If I can I will.'

## CHAPTER SIXTY FOUR

Lorraine walked out of court holding Luke's hand, her head high and a smile on her face.

'Told you it would be alright didn't I.' Luke said.

'I know, but the nerve of the cheeky bastard, trying to blame me and his other victims.'

'Yeah, well it's not something we haven't heard before.'

'Excuse me!' Lorraine said a moment later as a microphone was pushed in her face.

'How does it feel to be a hero, or heroine to be correct?' A young man with two days of dark designer stubble, asked.

Just stopping herself from retorting, ''Get that out of my fucking face, prat.'' she said. 'There will be press interview later on today thank you.' Then she and Luke hurried past the gathering press and flashing cameras.

Twenty minutes later they were walking up the steps of Houghton Police station, as they entered the applause started. Lorraine gasped as Clark patted her shoulder. 'Well done Lorraine.'

'Thanks.' She replied with a smile, she walked the gauntlet of smiling complementing comrades. Once in her office she slumped down in her chair. 'Wow, didn't expect that.'

'Well done pet.' Sanderson said.

'And well done from me too.' Dinwall said, as Carter nodded in the corner.

'Me as well,' Carter said shyly. 'I hear the creep had plenty to say for himself.'

'Thanks guys, and he so did Carter. But for now back to work, we still have this scalping bastard to catch.'

'To damn right we do.' Sanderson practically growled, as he left the room.

With a frown Lorraine stared at his retreating back; then it suddenly dawned on her why he'd been so grumpy lately.

'Shit.' Lorraine slapped her forehead with the palm of her hand. 'Shit, shit!' She had been so wrapped up with her own problem that she had failed to realise the reason for her old friend's attitude.

'What?' Luke asked, as he picked up some files from Dinwall's desk.

'Sanderson, he's due for retirement next year.'

'Is he?'

'Yes, that's the reason he's been such a bloody pain in the arse for a while now.'

'What the hell can we do?' Luke shrugged. 'I'll be sorry to see him go. But time...'

'Waits for no one,' Dinwall said. 'He gets on me tits most of the time, and I hate to say it, but I'll miss the old sod as well.'

'Wow that's big coming from you Dinwall.' Luke said.

Lorraine sighed. 'Well there's nearly a year yet, so nothing said, okay guys, we'll deal with it when it comes around, just cut him some slack, okay.'

## CHAPTER SIXTY FIVE

He waited at the bottom of the field for her, knowing she would not be happy if he waited in the yard like some of the other parents, after all, as she kept reminding him she was ten in a few weeks, and next year she would be in the big school down in Houghton, and hadn't those ten years flown by, one or two girl friends in the mix but nothing serious until he'd met Christina. Truth be told though, he'd actually known her for years, on a purely nodding acquaintance of course. Christina was very shy, that's why her father saying she had taken off into the blue yonder before, just didn't wash with him. They were even talking about actually getting married and she was spending more nights at his house than hers, so none of it made any sense at all.

The frustration of being entirely helpless was eating him up, he lay awake nights trying to work out what to do, if the authorities couldn't help him, then he was one man against the world because her father just shrugged his shoulders whenever he went over to see if she had been in touch.

'Dad…Dad…DAD.'

Jacko blinked and looked down at his daughter. 'Sorry pet, was miles away.'

'You were an' all…What you doing here anyhow I can walk home myself you know or with Suzy and Emma, it's just down the road.' Emphasising the fact that home was just down the road she pointed over towards the Seahills.

'I went for an echo, just thought I'd,' he looked at her puzzled expression. 'What?'

'Where's the echo?'

'Oh.' Jacko groaned. Not about to tell Melanie about his run in with Dev this morning, and his failure to call at the paper shop before coming to the school which was what he'd planned, Jacko shrugged. 'Forgot.' He grinned at her.

'I'll come with you if I can have some sweets, or a bag of crisps.'

Jacko fiddled with the change in his pocket. 'Might be able to manage a small mix-up, that's if you don't take the huff 'cause it's egg and chips for tea, seeing as your nana now thinks she's a world class bowling champ.'

'Is she?'

'Err…No. Mr Skillings won, remember.'

'She will be though won't she, cos nana won't let anybody

beat her, wont she not.'

'You're right there pet. God help Mr Skillings from now on.'

They passed Suzy and Molly who were playing on the swings.

'Hi Melanie,' Suzy shouted. 'I'm just waiting with Molly, till her mam comes.'

'Mum.' Molly giggled, which set Suzy off.'

'Okay, see you after tea.' Melanie waved.

'That the new girl?' Jacko asked.

'Yeah, she's alright...And I really love egg and chips.' Melanie nodded her head with conviction, as together they turned and headed back to the paper shop.

Ten minutes later and back home, Jacko opened his newspaper to find the face of a young woman staring out at him with the caption, 'DO YOU KNOW THIS WOMAN.'

For a moment his blood froze, he blinked and stared again, his breath catching in his throat.

Then disappointment flooded his body as he spotted the small birthmark under the woman's right eye, something Christina didn't have, also the top half of the picture was blurred so he couldn't tell by her hair, and her lips looked slightly fuller. Apart from that she was a dead ringer for Christina.

'Where the hell are you?'

## CHAPTER SIXTY SIX

'And just where the hell have you been?' Vanessa demanded, as Suzy and Molly came sauntering into the kitchen. 'I was starting to get worried, haven't you seen our Emma? I sent her out looking for you ten minutes ago.'

'No, never seen her. We were waiting for Molly's mam.'

'Mum.' Molly said, as they both started giggling.

'I take it you haven't found her?' Vanessa frowned at them both, as she remembered Sandra saying she had got into a car with two men.

'No mam, we went over hers and nobody's in. Can Molly have some tea?'

'Aye why not, shepherd's pie, there's plenty,' she smiled at Molly. 'Do you like shepherd's pie?'

Molly not ever remembering having shepherd's pie in her life before, nodded politely as Suzy said. 'Great, can we go back down the swings now?'

'Half an hour, that's all mind you.'

'Yeah.' They said in unison.

Vanessa shook her head as they walked out the door.

The girls skipped off towards the swings, passing Claire on their way. After she'd said hello Claire looked around, inside she was shaking her day had been filled with the beeps of her phone telling her there was yet another message. Stressed out in case her nightmare of two years ago was coming back, she had begged Kerry to go to the police when it didn't stop, only Kerry had said again that it would be a waste of time. They had argued, with Claire saying the police could trace where the messages were coming from, though Kerry wasn't so sure, she had agreed that if the messages hadn't stopped after Robbie's party then they would go, Claire wondered if Kerry was having as bad a day as she had.

Just about to close the gate she heard Darren yelling from the back garden, she reached the gate into the back when her mother came hurrying down the steps.

'What the hell's the matter?' Vanessa said. 'You'd think the place was on fire.'

'Look.' He yelled again, as he started pointing and kicking at something on the grass.

Both Vanessa and Claire stared at the ground where he was pointing. At first glance it looked like a bunch of red and white roses blooming low to the ground, but as they came closer they soon realised that someone had taken a pair of scissors to Darren's beloved Sunderland top.

Darren was in tears, it was the first time in his life that he had owned a Sunderland top. 'Who mam who?'

Vanessa put her arms around him. 'I don't know son, but we'll fucking well find out, the nasty gits.'

'But...'

'Never mind son it'll be some jealous nasty toe rag wishing he could play football like you...We'll get you a new one don't you worry.' At the same time she was wondering just where the hell she would get the money for a new one, because they certainly didn't come cheap, not even off the lifters.

Claire bent down and started to pick the pieces up as Vanessa led Darren into the house. Her phone beeped and she gasped. 'No again, please not again.'

## CHAPTER SIXTY SEVEN

Kerry was taking a short break and wondering aimlessly through Houghton, every now and then her phone would beep delivering another message. It had gone on all day, and if she could get her hands on the person responsible she would throttle him/ her.

If I switch my phone off then they've won, she thought sitting on one of the seats facing St Michael's church on the Broadway.

Maybe that's what they, he or she, want.

Me, cut off from everybody.

She looked around, people walking past, some in a hurry some just strolling, a mother not much older than Kerry with bright bottle red hair pushing a twin buggy. Kerry knew the girl and prayed she wouldn't look over, once Jemma Wardle got talking nothing would shut her up. She was nice enough just a total bore, every time she came into the shop, which was most days whoever was serving ended up with a long queue of not very happy customers. Quickly Kerry averted her head so as not to catch Jemma's eye.

Just as she did so her phone beeped.

Not again.

Who the hell?

She took her phone out and glared at it as if demanding that it should answer, but all it ever said was caller unknown.

'Hello Kerry, taking a break?'

Oh no!

Kerry looked up at a smiling Jemma.

'Hi Jemma,' she forced a smile on her own face and for the next fifteen minutes she was told over and over about the exploits of Jemma's two year old daughter Danielle's, reign of terror.

Just as she was about to politely escape, the strange young man who had came in the shop the day before, passed by.

## CHAPTER SIXTY EIGHT

Sadly Lorraine left the small house tucked away in a cull de sac near Seaburn beach, Luke quietly closed the door behind them. Getting into the car she shook her head at Luke. 'I so hate this part of the job.'

'I know,' Luke fastened his seat belt, before gently squeezing Lorraine's hand. 'Bad enough a young life stolen, but a stupid skate board accident,' He started the car and headed for home. 'Just wondering if it's a blessing to find out, pretty soon just what's happened.'

'Is it ever a blessing?'

'I suppose, well maybes, especially if you are possessed of a vivid imagination.'

'Must be hell.'

'Yeah I went through it with Selina, remember?' he grimaced as he used his left hand to rub his knee.

'Really you should go see the doctor if that's still bothering you...I promise he won't cut it off.'

Luke pulled a face at her. 'It's nothing really, it will mend.'

'So why isn't it?'

Luke shrugged then changed the subject. 'That reminds me Selina rang earlier, she isn't going to get back in time to make that meal she's been promising us, can we pick fish and chips up.'

Lorraine laughed, 'Guess its fish and chips for supper then.'

Fiona stared out of the window, noting that the lights were still on across the road, what lovely people she thought, taking my Molly in while I was at the hospital, and that bitch Hawkes can apologise till she's blue in the face, sending a squad car to watch the street because she couldn't get here while I was at the hospital, not good enough. Even if Oliver was only a few minutes getting in after Molly.

She closed the curtains, at least Liam was out of danger, a slight smile was on her lips then passed as quickly as it had appeared. But John and Martin, she sighed. Reliving that night, if only they had not seen the young man beaten to death, the casual way two men exchanged parcels of drugs while it was going on, the young woman's screams as she was dragged along the road, it had been like walking into a corner of hell.

# CHAPTER SIXTY NINE

Just after midnight, Danny said, 'Shit!' as he indicated a left turn to Penshaw village, when the police car which had been behind them since the roundabout at Shiney row, suddenly put its sirens on. He pulled up once he was round the corner, then heaved a sigh of relief as the police car sped on past.

'God, I thought he was after us.'

'Why we haven't got the grass yet?' Len said.

'Oh for fucks sake, it's the friggin middle of the night idiot, I thought he might be wondering what a bunch of blokes were doing riding around at this time of a night.'

'He might have been going to stop us but looks like an emergency came up, thank God.' Jacko said.

Danny restarted the engine. 'Okay, let's get it over with. See how much we can get tonight.'

Five minutes later they pulled up outside of the field. They drove along the track to the very edge of the woods. 'Okay, quick as you can.' Danny handed the spades out.

'Do you know I've got a blister?' Len said, taking the spade off Danny.

'Poor you. Dig with the other fucking hand then.'

'How?'

'For pity's sake Len.' Adam pushed him out of the way.

'Just saying.' Len followed them to the top corner where they started digging.

On with his second roll and still muttering on about blisters and nasty infections that he was sure to catch, which the others were ignoring, Len's spade hit something hard. 'Oww,' he yelled as the shaft of the spade sprang upwards, scraping the top off his blister. 'That bloody well hurt.'

Adam who was next to him laughed, the other two looked up.

'What's happened now?' Danny asked.

'Me blister's burst.'

'Come here I'll kiss it better,' Adam said, as Len scowled at him. 'Come to daddy.'

'Shut up.'

A moment later Len screamed again.

'What the fuck now?' Danny said.

'Shh.' Len, heart pounding, began to back away from the spot. 'It's a ghost.'

'I don't fucking believe it.' Jacko, staring at Len, dug his spade into the ground and rested on it.

'Friggin hell, he's finally lost it.' Adam shook his head in total disbelief.

'Shh.' Len insisted, as they all stared at him.

Then Adam cocked his head and leaned forward, in a long drawn out voice, he said. 'Is anybody there?' A moment later he collapsed in a heap laughing his head off.

'Will you stop taking the piss and listen?' Len yelled at them.

Shaking his head Jacko muttered, 'Unbelievable.'

'Hang on.' Danny held his hand up.

It was then that they all heard a very faint. 'Help me.'

'Shit,' Danny yelled, 'there's some fucker under here. Come on start digging.'

A minute later they all hit something solid with their shovels.

'Fucking hell,' Adam whispered. 'Some poor bastards been buried alive.'

Frantically they began scraping the soil away with their hands, on his hands and knees facing Jacko, Adam, whispered. 'What if its Farmer Macintyre's doing, we might be next?'

For a brief moment Jacko looked into Adam's eyes, then shrugged and continued scraping at the soil. Every now and then they heard 'Help,' in a voice which seemed to be getting fainter each time it was said.

Soon they were faced with a six by six stretch of wooden planks.

'Room for more than one in there?' Jacko said. 'Youse two start at that side. Come on Adam, we'll start here.'

After a couple of minutes they had all of the planks up. Thinking he was seeing double Jacko blinked. Two men, at least four feet apart were lying face up, one was staring at them tears ran down his face as he whispered. 'Thank you.'

He slowly lifted his arm, the other man didn't move. They helped the conscious man up while Jacko examined the first man's double. 'He's breathing, but only just, I think he's been hit on the back of his head, it's all sticky.' He wiped his hands on the back of his jeans.

'What happened mate, how the hell did youse end up here?' Adam asked.

Slowly the man shook his head. 'My, my brother...I didn't even know he was there...So quiet... Is he...Is he dead?'

Danny held up his hand. 'Believe me Adam we really don't want to know. Here's what we'll do. I'll phone an ambulance, then we'll get the hell outta here.'

'We can't leave them.' Jacko said. 'Fucking hell, it's not a pair of dogs we've dug up.'

'Couldn't leave them either.' Len nodded.

The man clutched at Jacko's leg. 'He's right, thank you, thank you...But go, go now...I won't tell anyone who you are, or what you even look like...Because really you don't want to be involved... My brother?'

Jacko sighed. 'He desperately needs help mate.'

'Okay,' Danny took his phone out, 'grab everything...Now.'

'The grass as well?' Len asked.

'Of fucking course!'

Not wanting to move the badly injured man, Jacko and Danny carried the first man towards the road where he would be seen by the ambulance and a few minutes later they were hiding in the van at the top of the bank anxiously waiting.

'I feel awful, fucking just leaving them.' Jacko punched the back of the seat.

'Aye mate, we all do. But he was right we had to go, God only knows what we might have got involved in if we'd stayed, we have our own family's to think of.' Danny said. 'And the other one, if it is a head injury you're not supposed to move them, we did the best we could.'

'Five minutes, five fucking minutes then we go back and take them ourselves to the fucking hospital.' Jacko emphasised his words with another punch at the back of the seat, while the other three silently looked at him.

Danny knew Jacko was capable of overtaking the three of them and going back for the two men, he wanted to himself, it went right against the grain to leave them, but he could see the bigger picture. And, if Farmer Mackintire was at the bottom of this, then his mate Mrs Archer would be in the mix somewhere.

A moment later he heaved a sigh of relief when an ambulance came down the lane from the other direction. 'That's it, time we were outta here.' Leaving his lights off he turned the van and headed for home.

FIVE HOURS LATER

## CHAPTER SEVENTY

She held her finger to her lips as she looked at Sarah and Marta. They both nodded and fell into step behind Christina; slowly they crept along the passage way towards the back door.

She had thought long and hard and knew deep inside it was now or never, if she did not at least try to escape then she would explode in the kitchen and attempt to stab one of them, a plan doomed to failure as she would be dead in seconds. More than one had gone that route.

At least this way there was a chance, however slim. Sarah had begged her to take her along, and this had aided her decision while the girl was still whole, because what had happened in the middle of the night had been a warning, showing her what was to come one more day and she would be nothing but a broken doll like the others. It was now or never, plus the latest baby had not been taken yet. If she could escape with the information she had, then lives would not only be saved but made whole again.

Like just about every one brought here she had rebelled more than once, she had been beaten over and over, with Draco, enjoying every punch, kick, that he dealt out, though he actually seemed to enjoy it more watching others inflict the punishment. She shivered as they reached the door. At five o clock in the morning she prayed that the out workers were all home safe and well.

Slowly she put the key in the lock, having first sprayed it with WD Forty, and praying that it would turn silently, she held her breath, and knew that behind her Sarah and Marta were doing the same. All of their hearts pounded as fear of being caught nearly overwhelmed them. Christina knew that if the key made even the slightest sound she would turn back and hide and her one chance would be gone forever. Never again would she be able to get up the courage to try again. Suddenly Sarah's legs gave way and she fell against Marta's side. Marta held her up, whispering in her ear. 'It'll be fine kid, we'll make it.'

The key turned without a sound and the door opened.

Turning to Sarah and Marta she mouthed. 'Thank God...Now.'

They ran, reaching the gate Christina pulled the bolt, suddenly they were free, and ran straight into the arms of four men armed with guns.

Christina took a deep breath, but a large gloved hand covered her mouth stifling any attempt at a scream. She fought the best she could, praying they would kill her quickly, and not caring if her scalp was to be the next one hanging on the wall. But her efforts were useless, and she was dragged and bundled into a car. She tried to look around for the others, praying that maybe just one of them might have made it.

Between sobs she struggled to sit up, someone was in the front seat staring at her.

Her eyes focused and she gasped. 'Lor...Lorraine Hunt!'

## CHAPTER SEVENTY ONE

The Blue Lion was surrounded by police. Luke gave the go ahead for the door to be broken in. 'Use the big red key and ram it. Steve...Go.'

Everyone stepped back; it took Steve, a very large Asian policeman, just one gigantic heave and the door shot open.

Within moments they were all inside. Three men ran up the stairs and searched the rooms, while Luke and four others did the downstairs.

Coming back down the stairs Steve looked at Luke and shook his head. 'Nobody up there.'

'Fuck! It's deserted down here too.'

'Tip off, you reckon?'

'God only knows...Search for anything, anything at all that could be incriminating, I mean anything.' He walked outside and leaned against the wall.

About to take his phone out, it rang and he nearly dropped it, grabbing at it, he caught the phone just before it hit the ground.

'Hello.'

'Great guns this end Luke, caught the bloody lot of them. And what a can of worms.'

'It's a no-go here, the place is deserted. Got the guys searching.'

'Shit, so the bitch got away?'

'Yup, it's looking that way.'

'Damn!'

FRIDAY

## CHAPTER SEVENTY TWO

Kerry stared out of the shop window, a frown on her face. He had passed the shop again-the stranger who had popped into the shop on Monday, only this time he had waved at her and mouthed. 'See you soon.'

'Who the fuck?' She muttered.

'Pardon?'

Kerry swung her head towards the counter. Mrs Henderson was glaring at her, holding an echo in one hand and a chocolate bar in the other.

'Sorry, thought I saw a duck out there, thought it might have wondered down from the Market place.'

'Aye right!' Mrs Henderson slapped a five pound note on the counter. 'You must be on something strong to be seeing ducks in the middle of Houghton.'

'What?' Kerry took a deep breath; the last thing she wanted was to lose her temper, then her job. 'Well I'm sorry if you thought I said something else.' She picked the five pound note up, took the change out of the till, and smiling handed it over.

Grumbling to herself. Mrs Henderson walked out of the door.

'Shit.' Kerry looked at her watch, half an hour to go, just then the manager came from the back room.

'You can get yourself away now Kerry if you want. I know you'll want to get ready for the party.'

'Oh that's great, cheers Gillian.'

As she was walking out of the door her phone beeped quickly she glanced at it.

SEE YOU SOON, in capital letters.

She gasped, there had been no messages for the last couple of days, Claire had not had any either, so they had agreed even though Claire had still wanted to, not to go to the police, or tell anyone, including their mother.

## CHAPTER SEVENTY THREE

Carter crept down the stairs and headed for the front door, he wa meeting Dinwall, Sanderson and a few others from work. Dinwal had thrown the gauntlet down and bragged that he could bea Carter at darts. But Dinwall didn't know that Carter was very goo and that he hoped to show the big mouthed git, just who was th best. He knew that Luke had put his money on him to win, so tonight he would play the best he ever had.

He reached for the front door and turned the handle only to find it locked with the key nowhere in sight.

'Oh friggin hell!'

'Is that you son?' His mother said, from the sitting room.

'No it's Batman,' he looked quickly around at the hall tabl for the keys. 'Shit.'

'What?'

'Of course it's me.'

'Come in here a minute.'

Carter's shoulders slumped. 'Really, do I have to?'

'If you want to get out of this house tonight, yes.'

He marched through into the sitting room and sat on the chair facing her. 'What do you want?'

'I want to know what it is you have to tell me, and why you have been avoiding me for most of the bloody week.'

Taking a deep breath, Carter said quickly. 'Mother I'm gay.' There, he thought, almost overwhelmed with relief, I've said it.

'Is that it?'

Carter looked at her in shock. 'What do you mean is that it?'

'Son I've known for years.'

'What?'

'I am your mother, of course I knew.'

'And...You're...You're not bothered?' Carter shook his head in disbelief. He had waited years to tell her, worried all that time what her reaction would be, and here she was calm as anything, saying she already knew.

'Son, you are what you are, and I'm proud to be your mother.'

Carter started to cry. 'Thanks mam.'

Leaning over she patted his hand. 'Now go wash your face, the keys on top of the mantel, and get yourself out, cos that new thriller's on the telly.'

## CHAPTER SEVENTY FOUR

'Very nice of Fiona to hang around until tomorrow, so the bairn can come to the party with Suzy tonight, isn't it?' Sandra said to Vanessa.

'Told you she was alright.'

'Aye and that hubby of hers looks like a bit of alright as well.' Sandra grinned.

'Keep your hands off.'

'As if.'

'Anyhow, that's not him, that's his twin, the hubby's in hospital.'

'What for?'

Vanessa shrugged. 'Don't know.'

'So how do you know?'

'The biggest gossip on the Seahills told me.'

'And who might that be?'

'Our Suzy, she's fairly overtaken our Emma.'

Both of them laughed as they picked up the boxes filled with party decorations.

'Oh look who's passing.' Sandra said, staring out of the window. 'It's Christina isn't it? Bloody hell, she looks as skinny as a rake!'

'I know poor sod.'

'Do you reckon the rumours are true?'

'Oh, keep forgetting, you've been away for two days and just got back this morning...How's your sister?'

'She's good now. Hobbling about on crutches, but her Jake is home today... So go on. Tell me.'

'Well...'

There was a loud knock on the door, interrupting their conversation. 'That'll be Danny.' Vanessa said. 'He promised to take us and the party stuff to the Beehive in his van you do know he calls it Elizabeth. Yes!' She jumped up and down, then rushed to the door.'

'Vanessa.' Sandra shouted.

'Tell you all about it on the way there.'


The Beehive was packed with friends and neighbours to celebrate Robbie's birthday, his best friend Mickey had been given the job of getting him there, although Robbie was not too keen on the idea, much preferring a pub crawl at Durham to celebrate.

'Well I've already told Shaun that we'll meet him there, and the others.'

'So give them a ring, tell them we'll meet up in Houghton.'

'But...err.' Mickey's heart sank, what the hell can I say to ge him there? Fuck!

'But what?'

Its Shaun man, he wanted to go there first, just for to see som of the, err...Old timers. You know him and Stephen have come u from Manchester.'

'Okay, whatever.'

Mickey hid a grin, as he breathed a sigh of relief. Thank God he thought, knowing Vanessa would have killed him, and Kerr would have jumped on the pieces, if he had not been able to ge Robbie there without telling him the truth.

Turning they headed towards the Beehive.

Mickey was relieved when he spotted Shaun and a few of th others standing outside smoking.

'Hi guys,' Robbie grinned when he and Mickey reached them 'One in here eh, then we'll hit the road okay?'

'Yeah.' they all said, grinning behind his back as the followed him in.

Once through the outer door, he turned left and stopped dea when he saw the banners proclaiming HAPPY BIRTHDAY, th room overflowing with balloons. And everyone he knew with nile on their faces, and they all started singing.

Robbie looked around in amazement. Everyone he knew was
1ere. He spotted a very happy Jacko and Christina, Mr Skillings
1d his gang, just about everybody he had ever known in his life.
[is heart swelled when his mother stepped out of the crowd and
ung her arms around him.

Everyone was smiling and still singing except Kerry, she was
)o busy staring in shock at Shaun. 'Oh fuck,' she whispered. 'It's
im.' Standing at the bar and facing her with a smile on his face,
`as the young man who had been in the shop, and stared at her
1rough the window half a dozen times this week.

She didn't know what to do, no way could she kick off and
)oil Robbie's birthday. She looked the other way, but out of the
)rner of her eye she saw him move closer. Suddenly he was right
i front of her.

'You don't recognise me do you?'

Keep cool. She thought, turning she stared at him, then slowly
1ook her head.

'Guessed you didn't...It's me Shaun...Shaun Broddy,
:member now?'

Kerry gasped. 'Never...You've changed.'

'Well it's been easily five, nearly six years.'

Kerry was suddenly flooded with memories. Shaun had lived

next door until her thirteenth summer, he was her first love, he first kiss, and then abruptly his folks had moved to Mancheste they had drifted apart, although she knew he still kept in touch wit Robbie who was the same age.

Feeling slightly embarrassed, something new for Kerry, sh smiled. 'Well good to see you. Didn't know you were comin tonight, how did you keep it from Robbie?'

'He knew I was coming up for his birthday, a night out wit the lads, but never suspected this.'

No way can it be him, she thought, he used to be a nice ki unless he's changed in more ways than one, quickly she looke around, nobody looked even remotely suspicious. He sat down the seat next to her.

Two hours later Fiona and Doris, took Molly, Emma, Melanie an Suzy, home, Suzy was to stay with them on their last night, an Emma was to have a sleep over at Melanie's.

And now getting on for midnight and just as the party wa winding down, Dev walked in.

'Good party? Bastards.' He yelled from the doorway.

The room fell silent as Vanessa pushed her way to the fron 'Out now, this is a private party. And you weren't on the frigg list. We don't want any trouble, so just go.'

'I'll deal with this mam.' Robbie slurred, pushing himself away from the bar to stand next to Vanessa.

'No son, it's alright he's on his way out.' She turned to Mickey and gestured with her head towards Robbie. Getting the message, Mickey and a couple of friends circled Robbie.

'Am I really, I don't fucking think so.' Dev curled his lip. 'Where was my twenty first birthday party...Mam?'

'What?'

'You heard right...Mam...I'm the one you gave away, remember me.'

'No...I'

'Yes you did.'

Some people quickly began to put their coats on to leave, the Seahills diehards however, craned their necks to hear what was going on.

A moment later Dev pulled a hand gun out and held it above his head. 'Nobody move.'

In shock, some froze, as others screamed, a few tried to hide under the tables.

'Shut up now...Don't anybody move or I'll kill the fucking lot of you,' he yelled. Silence fell like a heavy mist from nowhere covering the room as he transferred his gaze to Vanessa. 'You bitch, are going to pay for what you fucking well put me through, but not only you, the rest of the bastards you spawned,' he glared at Robbie. 'Especially him!'

Robbie lunged for him but his friends although terrified, held him tight, Dev laughed, then looked at Kerry; staring into his eyes she knew he was the stalker, her eyes still locked with his, Kerry silently stood up, beside her Claire and Shaun tried to pull her back down, but Kerry shrugged them off and took a step forward.

'Come on you fucking cow face.' Dev used his free hand gesturing her forward.

Out of the corner of his eye he saw Jacko stand up. Ignoring Christina's pleas for him to sit back down Jacko glared at Dev. Christina was devastated, she felt as if she had left one nightmare for another. 'Please sit down Jacko, she sobbed.

Jacko shrugged her arm off. 'You got the guts to use that?'

'You want to find out?'

'No please, please don't do this.' Vanessa begged, jumping in front of Kerry. 'Sit down Jacko for God's sake,' turning quickly to Dev, she begged. 'Just go, please go.'

'Again, is that all you can fucking say to me.' He pushed the gun in her stomach.

She screamed, along with everyone else, Robbie tried another lunge and was again held back. Dev laughed at him.

He turned back to Vanessa, his gun still firmly held against er. 'Why, the fuck for mam? 'He laughed. 'Come on bitch, tell me why? What's it to me if I blow your fine fucking family to bits.' He laughed even louder.

Darren had been on his way back in from the toilet, when Dev had come in through the other door way. Quickly he had ducked behind a chair, and now he took the opportunity to crawl outside. He kept on all fours until he was out of the main door, then ran as fast as he could across the road and started banging on the first door he came to.

Unaware that Darren had escaped, Dev went on. 'Or should I say my fucking family. That's a laugh, my family.' He laughed, high pitched and hysterical. 'Isn't fuck face?'

'Please don't do this,' Vanessa begged, 'you've got it all wrong, we'll get you help for whatever happened to you...I'm sorry,' her whole body was shaking as she pleaded with him. 'Please, don't do it.'

'Let me go,' Robbie struggled with his friends. 'I'll kill the fucking bastard.'

Ignoring him Dev laughed even louder as he glared at Vanessa. 'Sorry doesn't cut it bitch,' he brought his hand holding the gun down and pointing at the crowd, went on. 'Which one first, eh...Come on, who's first? Bastards. Come on.'

'No.' Sandra stood up and walked up to him.'

'Who the fuck are you to tell me no, fucking short arsed twat.'

'I'm your mother.'

'What?' he started to grin, 'think I'm gonna fall for that, dat bastard, outta the way now.'

'It's true.' Sandra looked at Vanessa. 'Tell him.'

Vanessa nodded. 'Yes she is.'

Vanessa had vowed to keep Sandra's secret years ago, but sh was pleased Sandra had come forward, because another minute an she would have told him herself.

He stared at Sandra, as did the twenty odd terrified people wh were there. He shook his head. 'No...No. I'm gonna kill the lot o youse bastards. Lie's all lie's.'

Mr Skillings leg suddenly gave way and he flopped into hi seat with a loud groan. The sound echoed around the room an broke the fear, people who had held their breaths suddenly gulpe and started screaming and running for the door.

'Stop it,' Dev yelled, panicking he looked at the fleein people. 'Stop.' Realizing that he was losing control he dropped hi hands and his head followed.

Seizing the opportunity, Robbie jumped forward and landed right hook on Dev's chin. 'Out, out.' He yelled, as Dev slowl folded inwards towards the floor.

Quickly Shaun and Mickey flung themselves on top of Dev, a

Robbie kicked the gun out of his reach.

Outside the others clung together behind the fence, hidden from the pub by the dip in the land, waiting for the sound of gunshot, but the next sound was that of police cars.

Vanessa, holding onto Kerry and Claire and managing to keep a devastated Sandra in the circle, scanned the crowd for Darren. Her heart flipped when there was no sign of him.

'Where's our Darren?' she yelled. 'Oh God he must be still in here.' Panicked she screamed his name. 'Darren.'

'It's alright.' Mr Skillings shouted from further along. 'He's here, look crossing the road now.'

'Shit, duck Darren, for fucks sake duck.' Vanessa yelled.

Running towards them, Darren heard his mother and tried to make himself a smaller target, he tripped and fell flat on his face in the middle of the road. Jacko ran to help him. Quickly, just as the police cars were pulling into the car park, he dragged him to the edge of the road.

Covered in blood dripping from his nose, and a large scrape on his left arm. Darren said. 'I phoned the coppers mam. They're coming.'

'Aw, son, son.' Tears running down her face, Vanessa cradled Darren in her arms, while the rest of the family and friends, muttering, 'Our hero.' Found a place to pat him on his back.

The police quickly surrounded the building, Luke took a bullhorn out of his car, putting it to his mouth, he shouted. 'Come out now with your hands in the air.'

Robbie came through the open door, put the gun on the ground then held his hands up and followed by Mickey and Shaun, moved away from the gun and trying to stop the trembling in his whole body proceeded to tell Luke where Dev was lying as Mickey fell against the wall and slid down, he was quickly helped to his feet by Shaun and one of the policemen.

Two hours later there was a knock on Vanessa's door. 'That'll be the coppers.' Kerry rose from the settee and made her way to the front door. She opened the door to find Lorraine and Luke standing there. 'Come in.'

Lorraine nodded. 'We're here to see Sandra. 'I'm told she' here.'

'Through there.' Kerry closed the door behind them.

Sandra, who had barely stopped crying, lifted her head to Lorraine. 'How...How is he?'

'Well, not good, at the moment he's under guard at the hospital where they have him sedated.'

'Was he gonna kill us all?' Sandra's whole body shuddered and Vanessa took hold of her hand.

'Well that's just it; it wasn't loaded not even a real gun, just a replica. His aim was to frighten you all, payback time; he kept repeating it over and over. Have you any idea why.'

Sandra looked at Vanessa. 'You tell her.'

Vanessa ran her tongue around her lips. 'Okay;' she took a deep breath. 'When we were thirteen, Sandra got pregnant; we managed to keep it secret. We,' she took another deep breath. 'We arranged with an aunt of mine, Jayne, who lived in Swindon for Sandra to have the baby at hers, we were supposed to be on holiday. Aunt Jayne registered it under my name; she said there would be fewer questions asked, as she had the same surname as me. Some friends of hers adopted it.'

'Hmm, do you know the name of the adoptees?'

Vanessa thought for a moment, 'I think it might have been Cally V...Vince, yes that's it, and Todd.'

'And where's Aunt Jayne now?'

'She...She died, years ago.'

'I see.'

'Can I see him?' Sandra asked.

'More to the point Sandra, will he want to see you?'

Sandra dropped her head and whispered, 'It's all my fault, all of it, what he did...Frightening everyone.'

'We were only thirteen Sandra.' Vanessa patted her friends

shoulder. 'Just kids.'

Lorraine sighed as she stood up. 'Okay, I'll let you know the outcome when the doctor says he's fit enough to be questioned.'

'Thank you.' Sandra said.

Kerry saw them out. In the car Lorraine turned to Luke. 'What a fucking mess.'

THREE DAYS LATER

# CHAPTER SEVENTY FIVE

Standing at her gate talking to Mr Skillings, or rather listening to Mr Skillings waffling on about his latest bowling win over his lady friends, Vanessa watched as a police car drove past, craning her neck to watch it she said, as it stopped outside of Sandra's. 'That it gotta go...Catch you later.' Mr Skillings stared after her as she quickly hurried along to Sandra's house.

The night before they had talked about what to say to Sandra's husband when he got back from Germany on Friday, and what to and how to tell Sandra's sons. Deciding together that the truth was the only way, they then went to Vanessa's AA meeting, and ended the night with fish and chips, watching the sun go down while they reminisced on their teenage years.

Letting herself in, Vanessa smiled at Lorraine and Luke 'Cuppa tea?' She asked, making her way to the kitchen, Sandra shot her a look and mouthed, 'Thank you.'

A few minutes later, Lorraine put her cup on the coffee table 'Well Sandra, you should prepare yourself because I don't think you are going to like what I have to say.'

Sandra clasped her hands together. 'Okay, just tell me.'

Looking at Vanessa, Lorraine asked. 'How well did you know your aunt?'

'Not that well, she came up about once a year, she was my dad's sister...She was funny, used to make us all laugh, didn't she Sandra?'

Staring at the carpet Sandra nodded.

'Well, from our enquires we've found out that, the people who she helped adopt the baby, sort of fell by the wayside got into drugs and worse. Both of them have been inside for a good five years up until now.'

Sandra felt the hairs on the back of her neck start to rise, dreading the worst she lifted her eyes to Lorraine.

'I'm afraid that the baby, Dev, was more than badly treated.'

Sandra screamed. 'No...Oh God, I'm sorry it's all my fault,' she began to tear at her hair. 'Poor baby, poor baby.'

Vanessa quickly put her arms around her, keeping her arms pinned. 'No it's not your fault.'

'Without going into too much detail, the young Dev, along with three others, two who have now taken their own lives, were passed back and forth between a paedophile rings. Regularly beaten and forced to do things for food. As he got older they were made to steal, whatever and whenever they could. At the age of twelve, Dev and one of the others ran away. They becam separated a year later after living it rough on the streets. Dev ha never seen or heard of the boy again.'

By now Sandra was sobbing uncontrollably. 'Does...Does, h really- hate me?' She managed between gulping for air.

'I'm afraid so Sandra.' Lorraine felt so much pity for Sandra but after spending time with Dev and listening to his story, she als felt pity for him.

'Will they lock him up?'

Probably there will be a custodial sentence, how long depend on the judge.'

Sandra gripped Vanessa's hands tightly. 'Will he let me se him? Will he?'

Lorraine shook her head. 'I don't know, at the moment he i still very bitter.'

Vanessa squeezed Sandra's shoulder. 'There is always hop Sandra.'

'Is there...Really.' She shook her head.

Lorraine stood up crossing the room she looked into Sandra' eyes. 'You were just a kid Sandra, you had no way of knowin what would happen, hopefully one day he will come to realis this...Without hope we would have nothing.'

## CHAPTER SEVENTY SIX

Well then, what started off a bad month finished pretty well, what do you think?'

Lorraine looked at Luke, and nodded. 'Yes I agree, loads of bad bastards locked up, with plenty of thanks to Hawkes I have to say. Also she was brilliant on that raid, thank God, her contacts were found in time. And she sussed out that the business contact was a con to get the brothers together at a certain place, although I think we should have know more about it in the beginning. Since an awful lot of it was on our patch.'

Luke nodded. 'And very brave of the brothers to still identify the villains, plus half a dozen more after everything that happened to them.'

Lorraine rubbed her right eye, before saying with a smile. 'I just wonder who the four guys were who rescued the brothers?'

'Well they've got to be locals, and your guess is as good as mine.' He grinned at her.

'After nicking half of Macintyre's grass, damn good of them to hang around and do what they did.'

'Just wondering if the van they used is called Elizabeth.'

This set them both off laughing.

'Can of pop?' Luke asked, standing up and heading towards the small fridge.

'Yes thanks.'

A few seconds later Luke put a can on Lorraine's desk, then suddenly went down on one knee.

'What!' she nearly squealed in shock.

Luke started blustering just as the door opened and Dinwall Sanderson and Carter poked their heads round the door.

Lorraine was staring at Luke her mouth open as he said, 'no no, me friggin knee went off.'

Not knowing if she was pleased or disappointed, Lorraine started laughing with the others.